Escape From Assisted Living

—w—

Joyce Hicks

This story is a work of fiction. The characters and events are from the author's imagination and do not depict real people or events. Similarities to real people are coincidental.

ISBN: 1492817732
ISBN 13: 9781492817734

To all my family who love to read and write and encouraged me to keep going.

1

No Tablecloths

Do I know this woman?

Betty felt a moment of vertigo after the oversized vehicle pulled into her driveway with her son-in-law Vince at the wheel. A woman she couldn't quite place opened the back passenger door, set a step stool on the driveway, and turned expectantly toward the porch.

Oh, yes. It's Sharon Lynne. Betty often forgot that these days her daughter kept her hair streaked with blond. "Highlighted," Sharon called it. Betty had tried to think of a way to tell her this didn't suit her coloring at all.

After crossing the driveway, Betty kissed the cheek Sharon offered. Then obediently she used the stool to climb into the car (or was it a truck?), sitting down on the back of her coat in a way that her head felt pulled sideways. There wasn't a thing she could do about it, once Sharon buckled her in.

A few minutes earlier, Sharon had sighed when she spotted her mother waiting on the porch of her duplex in what Sharon thought of as her duck pose—feet slightly turned out and arms tight to her sides, gripping her purse over her stomach. A blue hem showed at the edge of her Sunday coat.

"I'll bet she's wearing a corset, Vince, and we're only going for coffee and a sandwich."

Vince had not answered, having learned long ago not to offer any opinion about women's clothes.

"You're wearing your bouclé set," Sharon said once Betty was settled in. "Very dressy, for us, I'm afraid."

"This is an outing, dear," Betty replied.

Awake at six, Betty had had plenty of time to dress nicely for the outing. She had kept on her housecoat for her morning routine—breakfast with the crossword in the paper and her pills. Today she did a bit of hand washing, keeping her eye on the morning show on TV. The chatty anchors were always welcome guests in Betty's kitchenette. With a luncheon date today, Betty was in the mood to make it an event, though just at a restaurant without tablecloths. Not that she would think of complaining to Sharon about the slap-dash nature of these outings. No, she was not that kind of mother. Their monthly lunch was hardly worth a drive from Elkhart to the larger city of South Bend in search of tablecloths in north central Indiana.

Betty had shoved hangers back and forth looking for something to match her spirits. *Not an old pants suit, no.* A smart sweater and skirt of cornflower blue caught her attention among the navy slacks and print blouses. It was rather old but a very good label. She had hidden the receipt from Charlie, in fact, when she bought it at the Fashion Flair, a shop that had been gone for years now, as had Charlie.

True to her daughter's premonition, she had thought how a corset would give her waist a nice little nip-in. Then she put on some navy shoes with a miniheel and paraded in front of the mirror. With her eightieth birthday on the horizon, she decided to take stock objectively. She turned sideways and straightened up.

"No hump," she said with satisfaction. "But, look at that tummy, Betty. For shame." Like straightening a stack of books, Betty sucked in here and pushed out there until she was satisfied.

She took another turn around the room, sashaying by the mirror. What was it Oprah said? "You go, girl!"

At her dresser, she applied some makeup, not overdoing it, of course, just a touch of color on her cheekbones and a dusting of fine powder. "I'm not going to look like a harlot," she said thinking of a woman in her bridge group.

As she smoothed her hair, taking time to admire the remaining auburn strands, she fell into her usual expression—vague attentiveness. With the life in her head often more interesting than the one outside, she had the air of a person listening to music except with no visible device.

At the strip mall parking lot, Sharon placed the step stool again for her mother when she got out. Hunched over to steady the stool while guiding her mother's fingers to the safety handle, Sharon wondered for the hundredth, no thousandth, time if she was a good daughter.

Would a good daughter let her mother live alone?

Betty held Vince's arm as they zigzagged through the parked cars, giving her a chance to muse on her daughter's marriage. Vince was a nice man, really, just not what she had in mind originally for her Sharon Lynne. More to her liking would have been a doctor, or lawyer, or even a professor. There might have been a two-story colonial or enriching travel. Betty suspected at the time they married that he was a proficient lover, Vince D'Angelo of the James Dean insolent lip and curls. Today that lip was covered with a mustache, not too well trimmed, and he was bald as an egg. For Sharon, apparently, his niceness made up for these other things, and she had come to like him very well herself.

Once inside Café Olé, Betty tilted her head back to gaze at the giant overhead menus. As she tried to read across the panels, the choices in red, yellow, and blue chalk swam together, so finally she pointed to a cinnamon bun in the bakery case. Frosting dripped over its edges seductively.

Sharon urged her to get the daily special that rotated on a plate at the register. "Honestly, Mother, a cinnamon bun? Here's your chance at a decent meal. How about this smoked turkey sandwich with red pepper mayonnaise?"

"No, just a cinnamon bun. That will be fine for me."

Sharon could tell from the way her mother gripped her purse that it was no use arguing with her. Old people could get so adamant about silly things.

Betty had ordered a sandwich here once, and it was obvious that the people who made up these concoctions did not have dentures—you wouldn't dare open your mouth wide enough to take a bite. She had resorted to cutting it up, but the sourdough was so rubbery even this had been a chore. However, a gooey cinnamon bun was perfect, especially if dipped in coffee. That was another thing—it was hard to get just plain coffee at these places. So this time she ordered tea and then saw the girl get out a cup and saucer the size of that ride at Disneyland.

"Never mind the tea. Just a small paper cup of plain coffee!"

After a stop at the drink station where Vince squeezed a handful of lemon slices into ice water and added a half-dozen sugars, he carried his mother-in-law's tray to a table, helped her off with her coat, and plunked his wife's purse on an empty chair. He knew the routine for these outings and his place in them. Relaxed, the trio began to catch up on news. Sharon told how one of her colleagues that Betty knew had finally had her baby. Betty wondered about the name, and Sharon said it was Rudolf.

Vince looked up from his sandwich. "Who would name a baby Rudolf?" A bit of mustard hung off his mustache from biting into his monster of a sandwich. Betty was about to say she thought it was pleasantly old fashioned when Vince added, "Why not Dasher or Blixen? How would that be?"

"Well, they are Hungarian," Sharon offered, laughing.

Betty's thoughts drifted to Hungarians, and she heard her mother's voice more clearly than her daughter's across the table.

"Let's go down to the Hunkies to see if they have any sausage," her mother was saying.

The Hunkies were Hungarians who lived along a sharp curve on a gravel road. The children would come up to their car with produce or meat to sell, and Betty recalled that in spite of their own hardships, her mother often gave the children an extra dime. Later, "the Hunkies" simply meant the sharp curve in the road, so "Be careful of the Hunkies" was meant as a caution when taking the curve. Once Betty had said, "Watch for ice at the Hunkies, dear," almost causing an accident when Sharon turned to glare at her. Then, she had tried to explain all this history to Sharon.

"Why, that's a pejorative word, Mother, no matter what, like calling Vince a Dago."

Well, of course, Betty knew that. She had just wanted Sharon to picture the little wooden houses with their truck gardens and pigs of days gone by.

Several taps on her arm reminded Betty to focus on the people at her table. She knew she was inclined to drift off, even when Sharon and Vince were giving her an outing like this one.

"Have you been to visit Aunt Louise lately?" Sharon was saying.

"Yes, a week ago with Mabel. We got all mixed up and two, uh, young fellows showed us the way back to the main road." As soon as she said it, Betty was sorry. Now they wouldn't let her drive around with Mabel.

Sharon placed her hand over her mother's, rocking it back and forth as if scolding. "Lost? Oh, mother."

Betty felt the familiar, slender fingers and admired how nicely Sharon now kept her nails. Sharon grasped tighter, guiltily pleased how in advanced age her mother still had a pretty face and equally fearful that she might do something dumb.

"Ladies in distress, men to the rescue, Sharon," Vince said to cut off a lecture. He went on, "You be ready to relax tomorrow afternoon, Mother Miles."

"Yes, we're coming to clean your house for you," Sharon said brightly.

Betty put down her cup. At Sharon's, no shoes were allowed indoors, and Vince ate his snacks at the kitchen table. They would be stacking her dishes in the cupboard, criticizing her cheerful throw rugs, and complaining about the plastic containers she kept on the counter.

"Oh, no, you don't need to," Betty said, opening and shutting the clasp on her purse.

"You can watch TV while we work," Sharon said.

"I never watch TV." Betty opened her purse again, got out her wallet, and then remembered these places had you pay ahead of eating, as if you might run off. Vince had already paid anyway, she thought next. This was their month to treat.

Vince smiled at her. "You do too watch TV. You watch that mean Judge Judy every day at three." He walked around the table, piling up their cups to carry over to the waste area.

"Well, maybe once in a while."

Betty looked at Vince more critically. He still had some life in him. Maybe he used those pills like those guys on TV who made love to their wives in all sorts of strange watery places. She almost giggled, then quickly composed herself. Sharon would be so horrified if she could see inside her mother's head. Indeed lately, Betty had found her thoughts taking her to new places and ideas.

"Mother, it won't take an hour. Vince can take out the trash, I'll vacuum, and you can dust," Sharon said, hustling Betty into her coat. When Sharon was on a mission, there was no stopping her. More objections were pointless, but it occurred to Betty that maybe Vince would sit down to watch *Judge Judy*.

They took the long way home, so Betty could see the progress on a shopping center development. Sharon also pointed out a new assisted living facility. Betty felt mildly annoyed by this pairing of tour sites. If Sharon thought she was ready for an assisted living place, she certainly wouldn't be hiking around a shopping center.

"Will you look at that," Betty said as they drove slowly by the facility that to her looked like a Midwestern hospital masquerading as a Florida resort.

Hopeful at her mother's interest, Sharon ordered, "Turn in, Vince." Perhaps her mother would take in the bird feeders in front and white rocking chairs on the porch.

But Betty was studying a sign meant to discourage traffic. "'Shady Grove Assisted Living. No outlet,'" she read aloud slowly. "Ha! You can say that again."

Vince laughed.

Sharon sighed. "Okay, Mother, you win."

Vince made a u-turn and headed out of the drive. When they got back to Betty's duplex, the step stool came out for the fourth time.

"Mother, put your left hand, not your right, on the door as you step down."

Betty groped with her right foot until she found the step stool. Sharon steadied her right arm until she took a heavy step to the ground with her left foot, tilting slightly off the edge of her shoe.

Sharon found herself short tempered with her mother's ineptness in getting out, though Sharon knew the SUV wasn't the ideal vehicle for transporting an elderly person, but she and Vince couldn't arrange their whole life around her, after all.

"If those shoes are that loose, they're worn out, Mother. Why aren't you wearing the new ones I got you?" She had brought home three pairs recommended by the podiatrist's office for her mother to choose from.

"Oh, I forgot about them," Betty said, though she knew perfectly well why she hadn't worn them. "Old lady shoes," she had said when Sharon left them by her couch. They were putty colored and heavy. Each foot felt encased in concrete when she had them on and looked that way too.

Feeling guilty now about her outburst, Sharon kept her arm around her mother a moment longer than necessary on their way to the porch. Was her mother getting fleshy? Sharon made a mental note to call the senior center to ask about the transportation to Senior-cize on Tuesdays and Fridays.

"Bye, Mom. We'll have a girls' day out soon." Sharon gave Betty a quick kiss as she unlocked the door for her and handed her house keys back. In the car, Vince was whistling and quickly put a pink business card back in his pocket when Sharon returned.

"Do you think she had a good time?" she said.

"Absolutely," he said, pulling out of the driveway. "Where to now?"

"Home to drop me off. I have a flan demonstration tonight, so your dinner will be on a plate in the fridge. When will you be home from work?"

"I guess about nine," he said vaguely. "I have to check on a job."

"At night? Can you bring in that big box later when you get home?" She pointed to the garage and went in the house as Vince wheeled out of the drive.

With nothing else on her horizon, Betty changed out of her good clothes and set a kitchen timer for forty minutes, just the right length of time for a nap. This was something else she did that drove Sharon crazy. *You don't have to set the timer. Just sleep as long as you want.* But the ticking of the white timer had a pleasant busyness about it, and it was comforting to know she would be summoned from sleep. Edging around what she called the "electric chair," another of Sharon's ideas, Betty headed for her own favorite armchair. She put her feet on an ottoman and tipped her head back for her nap, leaving the power recliner to nap by itself.

With the timer tick-ticking, Betty nodded off, and then sensed she wasn't alone in the room. Someone was in the recliner. It was Judge Judy! She recognized her little white collar immediately. The judge was glaring at her.

"Your daughter says you owe her twenty-five cinnamon buns, and you have throw rugs. Is this true?"

"I did eat cinnamon buns, but—" Judge Judy would understand when she explained about the restaurant without tablecloths where teenagers built giant sandwiches and about the chilly floors at home.

"Just answer yes or no!"

"Yes, Judge."

"What's a woman your age doing with throw rugs?" barked the judge. "Don't you know they're hazardous?"

Then Betty suddenly realized Sharon Lynne was there too, twisting the edge of her sweater, a pink Easter one with rabbits on it. Judge Judy addressed her, "And as for you, can't a woman have a cinnamon bun if she wants one?"

Betty was glad to see the Judge was on her side.

Then the judge continued to Sharon, "I'd go easy on the highlights, if I were you, honey. It looks cheap."

Sharon hung her head.

Wait a minute! No one should talk to her Sharon Lynne that way. Betty grabbed the controller for the electric chair and mashed the black button toward "Up." Judge Judy began to rise. She tried to grip the arms of the chair as the seat rose and slanted to dump her on her feet like a load of gravel.

"I'll be over to vacuum tomorrow!" she screamed. "So be ready!"

Ding! Betty's eyes flew open. The living room was empty. The electric chair was squatting quietly in its corner. As Betty carried the timer back to the kitchen, she thought again how handy it was, while she stepped carefully over the edge of her sunflower throw rug. She stopped to study the yellow rug that never did lie flat. Then she rolled it up to tuck it under the bed and even tossed a stack of margarine containers from the kitchen counter under there too for good measure. Next came some dusting. She touched up the old photo of Sharon in her pink sweater. She gazed at the sweet, serious face—there was a slight rumple in her forehead between her eyes as if something behind the photographer didn't quite suit her. Betty pressed it to her cheek and held it at arm's length. There was her dear girl, a hailstorm and rainbow together. What a time they had had together! She took up the heavy framed picture of her husband.

"What do you think, Charlie, Sharon Lynne thinks she should clean my house. Remember her room?"

Finally, Betty lugged the vac out of the closet and sat down on the ottoman to change the bag, putting newspaper down first. "I wouldn't want Sharon Lynne to have to tussle with this," she said. "Not with those pretty fingernails."

2

The Price

Wednesday was card day at the senior center, and Betty rode over with her neighbor Mabel. Since Mabel always gripped her arm wherever they went, Betty wondered if she could really see well enough to drive. So Betty kept up a monologue about the road as they went.

"Here we come to a stop sign," she declared as if it were a major point of interest.

"I can see that." Mabel slowed down a bit and made a sloppy turn to the right.

"Will you look at that, a kid on a bicycle? Better give him plenty of room." Betty crossed her fingers, and the bike sped up just enough to get ahead of them as they banged over the curb into the parking lot of the senior center.

During cards no conversation developed because this was serious business, but afterward one of their regular subjects came up—who is poorly, whether your husband is poorly, and what you are planning to do when you get poorly.

Ardyce, whose blue-grey finger waves were sharp as dents, described in excruciating detail the home addition her son had built.

"Yes, they've already got a nice place for me at the back of the house." She sketched it out on the score pad. "You walk right into my TV area with a little kitchen unit on the side. There's just a stovetop, but I'm sure I can use Frannie's oven anytime. I'll have a fridge, of course, and two, no, three cupboards. Now, the bathroom is—" Her account was interrupted when her phone rang. "My son," she mouthed as she stepped away from the table.

"I bet Frannie keeps that door to her part shut like a tomb," Bernice muttered. The other women shushed her.

Irene reminded them of her down payment on a condo in a premier Florida retirement community. "Pools, golf courses, and shopping, all right on the grounds like a swank resort." She described how the residents drove around in golf carts. "It'll be a hoot," she concluded.

"That's fine for you," said Bernice tapping Irene's dinner ring with its bulging diamond. "Not all of us married for money. Twice. Personally, I couldn't make even the monthly maintenance fee on a layout like that."

They then hashed over the merits of a condominium versus a retirement community.

Ardyce said she couldn't stand being around old people. "Gums, gas, and gossip. That's what you get with just old people. I won't have to worry about that since I'll be with family." From a fat flip album in her purse, she showed a photo of two grandsons holding a trophy and one of a little girl in face paint.

She paused, then went on, "By the way, did you hear that Mindy's daughter is back at home with her? That ob-gyn husband they were so proud of took up with his nurse, the one with the waggley rump." Heads nodded—they knew all about how doctors carried on.

"How about you, Betty?" said Irene returning to their musings. "You have a daughter. Has she got room for you, when you need it?"

Betty supposed Sharon and Vince had room, but room wasn't exactly the issue. She wasn't sure she could stand them, well, unless perhaps she was a stroke victim, and then she surely wouldn't want to be there expecting them to take care of her. In addition to her day job at the hospital, Sharon was a cookery appliance demonstrator. Her kitchen was full of little gadgets—knives, apple peelers, slicers, dicers, dippers, and dabbers. In the cupboard, arranged in gradu-ated sizes, was every kind of baking dish, custard cup, and soufflé dish. Then there were measuring devices—scales, cups, spoons, and Betty didn't know what all. She could just imagine living there would be awful, much as she loved her Sharon Lynne. Supposing she went into the kitchen to make some tea or even get a glass of juice.

"Mother, what do you need?"

"I'm heating up water for tea."

"Oh, here let me get out the teapot for you."

"But this pan works fine. I just need some hot water."

"But this will work better. Did you know, if the water boils for just one minute, you get a better infusion?"

And so forth. Maybe even Vince wasn't allowed to fix a simple sandwich in their kitchen, because she had observed he had his own cupboard with a few mismatched plates and some coffee cups. Living with them would be just too much. She and Sharon Lynne would begin to hate each other.

So Betty said, "I'm all set where I am in my duplex."

"Really, Betty," Irene went on, "you're obviously avoiding the issue. You should plan ahead because you just never know. Some little TIA event will turn into a big stroke, and there you'll be with no plans."

Betty suspected that Sharon had thought this over too, but it wasn't something they had actually talked about. Rather like sex. Everyone did it at some point, but you didn't talk about it with your daughter. At least, she and Sharon didn't. Sharon was a social worker at the hospital, whose job was to help families decide how to take care of their mothers and fathers. It was so easy for Sharon to go down the checklists with other people, showing them the best way to make a decision. Yet Sharon and she had never taken any of these steps. In fact, Betty wondered if the checklists really worked well with other families either once they stepped out of the office.

Conversation at the senior center turned to another favorite subject: narrow escapes.

Ardyce picked up this thread after another phone call, which was from her other son (she wanted them to know). "Did you hear about Mary Grace Webber's neighbor?" Her three companions had not heard. "She was found lying at the bottom of her basement stairs. Been down there twenty-four hours."

"No! Dead?"

"Well—" Ardyce began but the chatter cut her off.

"Is she that heavy-set woman with the poodle? I always say a little dog can get under foot more than a big one."

"Yes, I know her. I see her at church. Is she dead?"

"She went down to get some of her canned pickadilly, her ankle twisted, and her head hit the last step like a muskmelon and—"

"I didn't see an obituary."

"Not in my paper either. Now, when was this?"

Ardyce slapped down her phone. "She's not dead! She laid there with broken bones until Ray Hubble peeked through the back-door window and saw her."

"Hubble, the funeral man?"

"Yes, it seems he was a friend of hers from way back," Ardyce explained. "I heard they had an arrangement. If her house was dark more than a day, he was to come on in to find her."

"Out looking for business, I would say!"

"Well, it paid to have someone checking. Think of just lying there, her and her poodle. She said Precious never left her side," Ardyce concluded this tale with a flourish.

Betty snickered. "Guess you would call that *full service*."

The women all laughed, but contemplation of death-by-pickadilly sent a little chill through the group.

While the women were at cards, Sharon was at work on the other side of town at the hospital. An errand took Sharon through the neonatal department, but she no longer paused there to look at the infants. A few years back she had stopped her practice of picking out a baby that looked like it could be hers and Vince's. By now she had schooled herself to glance with the same dispassion as looking at pretty merchandise anywhere.

In spite of her mother's reservations, she had married Vince right after her senior year in college. They had met at a disco in South Bend where Sharon occasionally went with other girls from the small women's college she attended. The disco attracted the local boys, students at the colleges, or young men already working. Vince and Sharon had struck up a conversation and had met several Saturday nights at the disco before he ventured on the women's campus to pick her up. He was more attractive than she deserved, she felt. She knew other girls turned to look at them when he came in his Impala to get her. Who would have thought that a muscular, curly-headed guy with liquid brown eyes would choose her!

Though her mother never said anything outright against Vince, Sharon saw the little tension line around her mouth when he came over to her house in Elkhart, especially when his grammar wasn't perfect or he went into detail about his family. Her father, on the other hand, liked Vince for being a man's man, someone with interests like his own, carpentry and electronics. Sharon could care less about these, though she did have her father's capacity for care and detail. She was majoring in social work and had planned on going to graduate school, but the relationship between her and Vince held tight in spite of her mother's disapproval and her father's approval.

The secret was that Vince had made Sharon feel confident in a way that her parents had not. For them, the most ordinary occurrence could start a cosmic chain reaction that could snatch her from them. A thunderstorm far across

Lake Michigan could cause an undertow while she was at Benton Harbor beach with her friends. They would go out too far. Sharon could be swept away. Escaping that, on their return trip, a deer could cross the toll-way in their path, so they must return before dusk, the prime time for accidents according to her father, who sold insurance. Sharon felt like a precious, single peach guarded against the slightest breeze that might shake it prematurely from the tree. In short, she felt responsible for their happiness. But with Vince, it was different. He looked out for her, of course, but he didn't set such store by her that his love was a burden. And he was handsome to boot. So, what was the point of looking for someone else?

As it had turned out, Betty had been right that Sharon's choice of Vince came with a price, and it wasn't a missing DDS, CPA, or PhD. It was children. Sharon knew that her failure to conceive wasn't her fault. It was his, though she never actually told him so.

After years of misplaced elation over late periods, they had driven all the way to a clinic in Indianapolis. When he finally agreed to this solution, Vince waded through ten-page health questionnaires and obediently complied when ordered to fill vials. Looking politely into space, he even held Sharon's hand while she underwent procedures, her feet in stirrups.

However, when the test results were ready, Vince was bed-bound with a back injury. Braced for hormone therapy, surgery, or whatever else was necessary, Sharon waited, flipping through a parent magazine in the waiting room.

"Right this way, Mrs. D'Angelo. Where is Mr. D'Angelo today?" The assistant asked as she led the way to a pleasant room with a desk and chairs where the physician had their records laid out. Photos of many babies lined the walls.

Naturally, Sharon was stunned to hear that Vince was the problem, an exceptionally low sperm count. His virility wasn't going to count where it was needed the most!

"We can do some other tests and suggest some procedures he could try. But I must tell you, the odds aren't in your favor for conception." The doctor spoke kindly and offered counseling services related to marital relations.

"I'm not sure Vince would want to, well, talk about that." Sharon thanked the doctor and hurried to her car.

Then she had pulled into a parking lot and stared out her car window for an hour after this astonishing news. If he had been with her, he would have gotten the news from the specialist. Now, she would have to tell him herself. She wasn't sure how he would take this news, given that he hadn't wanted to go through the tests to begin with. He had rather old-fashioned ideas about what men did and didn't do. *Real Men Don't Eat Quiche* wasn't far from the truth in his thinking.

When she got home, she discovered he had forgotten she hadn't just been at work. He pulled her onto the bed with him, laughing at his own awkwardness.

"Come here, Sharon. It's a bitch just lying here all day. Can't go to work, can't even put my pants on." He had reached for her hand to pull her down beside him. "Can do this though. Let's make some music," he said, beginning a familiar routine. "I feel like this could be our lucky one. Pretty soon you'll be singing 'Rock-a-Bye Baby.'"

"Vince, probably not," she had said but fell into the rhythm of their moves. However, after he had forgotten her appointment, this time the proficiency of his lovemaking planted a small, resentful voice in her mind. Later, she went into the bathroom and turned on the shower to cover her anger and disappointment.

When Vince heard her sobs behind the noise of the water, he remembered her appointment with the specialist. Her tears could mean only one thing—she had some problem that couldn't be fixed. *Poor Sharon.* He would be extra caring of her, and they would be all right, kids or no kids. Emerging from the bathroom, Sharon didn't have the heart to tell him right off about the test results since he was feeling helpless. Somehow later the right moment never came.

It wasn't as if there were no children in their lives. Vince's family produced a dozen nieces and nephews. Holidays were raucous and crowded, when adults and kids laughed and argued with enthusiasm. Since Vince was a favorite uncle undistracted by his own children, he was always called on for football, video games, or shooting baskets in the driveway.

Sharon stayed with the women. They treated her politely, always being highly complimentary when the party was at her house. "Without kids you can keep things out like those candlesticks."

Of course, they assumed the lack of kids was by choice, she thought, *her choice.* This made Sharon even more standoffish with their children and apt to straighten up her countertops with a vengeance during a party.

3

Counter Moves

*B*etty settled on her couch with her mail—an advertisement, her utility bill, two solicitation letters—"gimme
letters" Betty called them—and an envelope that announced,
"You may already be a winner."

Well, this had some possibilities. Sharon said filling these
out was pointless, but Vince said it didn't hurt anything, you
never can tell. Betty went with Vince on this one and got out
a pen. She had to put her name in several spots, scratch off
her secret number that she was cautioned to save, check the
box declining magazine subscriptions, choose which sports
car she preferred in the event that instead of being the BIG
winner she was a runner-up, and pack various slips back
into a rather small return envelope. She would mail it along
with her utility bill later.

Next she flipped open what looked like a magazine, but
it turned out to be an ad for Shady Grove, RETIREMENT AT
ITS BEST—"Your quality living is our commitment." Betty
pressed her thin lips into an even thinner line; anything
that talked about "quality of life" was just covering for talk

about "quality of death." She got a new advertisement every week. Sharon had seen to that—Shady Grove, the Oaks, the Birches. Why were they named after trees? A memorial to what had been removed to make way for the establishment? There was some irony in that, Betty was sure.

She flipped through the glossy pages—friendship, activities, community dining room, wellness, and fun. But Betty wasn't taken in one bit. Then she paused over a photo of a congenial pair, mother and daughter, sitting at a round table set with teacups, sugar, and creamer. They seemed to be looking at a photo album, laughing companionably. Here was a mother who cooperated with her daughter's wishes and took herself off to assisted living without a fuss. No more taking mother shopping for groceries, picking up her prescriptions, or taking her to the beauty parlor, because all these needs were met by the caring staff.

Of course, these were only models in the photo, but still the picture of even pretended companionship made Betty feel sad today because of a little incident a few days ago. She had been having a nice chat on the phone with Sharon about their new countertops and suddenly everything had turned sour. They hadn't spoken since. Betty shook her head thinking of it again. She hadn't said a word of criticism, not *a word*, and Sharon had practically hung up on her.

Sharon had been describing how the installers had put finishing touches on her granite countertops. These were a result of a Parade of Homes she and Sharon had toured. Betty had been so pleased the way they had strolled arm in arm around the cul-de-sac of enormous houses open for viewing. She had noticed that the kitchens had been the attraction for her daughter with their six-burner stoves and granite countertops. Though Betty thought granite was more practical for tombstones and courthouses than countertops, she would never say so. After one nice plate slipped on its way to the cupboard, Sharon would regret her choice.

On the phone Sharon said, "I'm so glad we pulled out that old island unit with the bar stools. The granite is just stunning. You'll have to come over, Mother. I want you to be the first to see it."

"It's wonderful you can afford that luxury, dear," Betty had said, thinking how well Vince had provided for Sharon in spite of her initial impressions of him. On this project, he had put in a lot of time moving all the plumbing and adding another window in the kitchen.

"Redoing the kitchen is not a luxury, Mother. The old countertops were here when we bought the house." Sharon's voice had taken on an edge.

"Your house was certainly a good buy, dear. I always liked that speckled laminate." Sharon had done up the kitchen cleverly with red and blue gingham curtains. Betty wondered where she got her artistic sense, certainly not from her parents.

"That laminate was awfully dated, Mother. Why do you always think things should be worn to shreds before making a change?"

"I just meant your kitchen looked nice before." Betty tried to speak cheerfully to defuse the emotion she could hear building in Sharon's voice.

"I'm trying to make improvements in the house, Mother. It's not like, like," Sharon struggled to find the right words, "throwing money down a rat hole, as Daddy used to say. I always hated that expression."

Yes, Charlie had been tight with the dollar, Betty knew very well. She still recalled a huge argument over Sharon's request for white Keds when her blue ones were still perfectly good, according to him. Betty had gotten the white shoes the next day, and told Sharon to keep them at school.

Now, knowing how much store Sharon set by her kitchen, Betty felt glad Sharon could redecorate and continued spryly, "Of course, it's not wasteful spending, Sharon Lynne. I was only saying that it's wonderful you can start over again like that, just for fun."

"It's not just for fun!" Sharon said curtly. "New countertops are not a luxury! I can't demonstrate appliances without a good-looking kitchen, Mother." Sharon placed emphasis on the final word. "You never remember about my business."

Betty agreed hastily, "Of course not, dear. I mean, of course, I do remember." She was about to reassert that the kitchen must look lovely now, but Sharon hung up with hardly a goodbye and no arrangements offered to come over to see the improvements.

It felt awful to have Sharon Lynne mad at her. Charlie hadn't seemed to mind when their daughter got steamed over something, but for her it always felt like the end of the world.

Why didn't I say right away that the kitchen must look great?

Instead, she had said something about the old countertops, not that this should be so bad, really, but Sharon Lynne—oh yes, she was supposed to call her *"Just Sharon"*— was so sensitive. As Sharon's mother, she should remember this.

Betty put down the Shady Grove advertisement. She felt like talking to her daughter right now. Maybe she could put things right, and she got halfway to the phone. But would calling her be a bother? Besides Sharon would be at her hospital job now anyway and not even at home to answer the phone.

She walked around her living room, kitchenette, bedroom, and back to the front door. No sounds crept in from next door. Nothing was happening out on the street, not even a dog being walked. She thought about Mary Grace Webber's neighbor and her poodle waiting for rescue. It was way too early to go to bed, not even six o'clock. She flipped on the TV: an oil painting program, a home decorating show, golf, NASCAR, a woman selling vitamin tonic. Betty watched for a few minutes.

Even Shady Grove might be better than this.

It cost, of course, but she didn't need to be A GRAND PRIZE WINNER to live there. Her duplex, which had been modest enough at purchase, had appreciated, and she had made quite a profit on their house when she decided to sell it. Charlie would have been astonished that the bungalow he considered a money pit had been considered a perfect Arts and Crafts period home when it sold. She would have enough to move to Shady Grove. Maybe she owed it to Sharon and Vince to not be such a burden. Well, she could at least take a look at it. She supposed Sharon would tell Vince that at last her mother is being *sensible*. She would say something like, "I told you she'd come around to the idea." Perhaps once at Shady Grove, she and Sharon could be like the women in the picture.

Actually, Betty's call the next day suggesting they visit Shady Grove started a minor argument at Sharon's.

"Mother has agreed to visit Shady Grove, Vince." He was out in the yard, scraping some loose paint on the fence gate. He stooped down to get the underside.

"Are you listening?"

"Yep." He rolled onto his back to wedge the scraper better.

"So isn't that good news?"

"I think she's all right where she is."

Sharon knew Vince liked going over to her mother's duplex. Her mother's reservations about Vince had melted to such an extent that Sharon sometimes felt excluded. He would find reasons to go over and end up watching TV for a whole afternoon. She had even found him dead asleep in the elevating lounge chair, his face boyishly relaxed.

"Suppose she falls, like that woman in the paper? Then what, Vince?"

"Well—"

"Are we going to have her move in here with us? With a broken hip? Which one of us can stay home to take care of her?" Sharon pictured turning the den into a bedroom with one of those unsightly hospital beds in direct view of anyone coming in the front door.

"Maybe we should just wait until she falls to figure that out."

"That's you all over," Sharon said, barely keeping her temper under control. "Mr. Wait-and-See about anything important." Vince continued scraping.

"I won't force her to sign anything. I'll just try to make her feel it's her idea." Vince knew this technique all right. It had worked plenty of times on him.

"Well, see what she thinks about it," he said, cramming the scraper hard on a picket, creating a dent.

Returning to the kitchen, Sharon watched Vince for a few minutes through the new window. Even though she wished he were a little more communicative, she knew how lucky she was that he was helpful with her mother. She wiped up a tiny spill near the sink, enjoying the cool elegance of the counter and the track lighting she had chosen. The angled fixtures would create a perfect setting for a cutlery demonstration. The contractor's bill lay open near her and she glanced at it. *I could have gone with something less than granite.* Maybe it was extravagant. She ran her hand over the counter again, the surface still chilly even though her hand had rested there.

She stood awhile longer at the counter now thinking of her mother. Perhaps she was wrong in her assessment of her mother's situation in the duplex as unsatisfactory. But Betty would be less isolated in a facility with people to talk to. If she didn't appear for dinner, someone would go check on her. Sharon pondered what would it feel like not to have the little bubbles of anxiety (or was it guilt?) that floated upward and burst into her thoughts during the day? Or what would it feel like if she herself were an entirely good person who wanted her mother to live with her?

4

A Snap Decision

Sharon had volunteered to use her day off for an official visit to Shady Grove. Betty surveyed her closet to prepare for this event, an outing that merited a careful wardrobe choice. The brochure showed a dining room with chandeliers, so perhaps she should dress up. No, it wouldn't do to look too well off. One never knew how they priced these places. On the other hand, nothing too baggy either, as if she had a bathroom problem. She chose something she regarded as sporty, navy slacks and a sweater with cardinals embroidered on the front, and she even dared to wear the navy shoes in spite of their rather worn treads. A woman with birds on her sweater looked appropriately fun and grandmotherly for Shady Grove—though as it happened Sharon and Vince had produced no children.

Betty was pretty sure they had wanted a family. Sharon had gone through a spell of having a number of doctor's appointments at one point in her thirties. Betty had fussed about this until Sharon had assured her that she didn't have cancer or anything terrible. So she hadn't asked her point blank whether the mysterious appointments were about getting pregnant, but she had hoped to see some positive results. None ever turned up, and Sharon took on more responsibility in her department at the hospital. Then about five years ago, Sharon had begun with the cooking gadgets.

Since Vince was working days now, Sharon drove them in her sedan that required no step stool routine. Her grip on the steering wheel helped keep her inner tension in check as she hoped against hope that these professional people would say the right kinds of things. Too effusive and Betty would see right through the whole thing—first the small apartment in assisted living, then maybe a move to memory care, with a final move to skilled care, if necessary in the future.

"Mother, did you bring your bank statement?"

"I have everything I might need right here." Betty gripped her navy purse to her chest.

Sharon glanced at the square bag. Yes, it was large enough to assume her mother had packed it with the necessary documents, though she wasn't a rush-into-it kind of person. If she saw a dress she liked, she always had it held for a day so she could think about it, even at mall department stores. Moving the handbag from Betty's lap to the seat, Sharon noticed that the strap was cracked. Now, how old was that bag? At least ten years! She made a mental note to replace the ugly bag and sighed; her mother's thrifty inclinations might be embarrassing in the upcoming interview, though she had worn a newer outfit, thank goodness. Would Betty fit in very well at Shady Grove? Perhaps she should have steered her to another residential facility, one with more Medicaid residents.

The tension in the car suddenly reminded Sharon of her own first encounter with group living. When she was twelve, her parents had sent her to camp for the month of her mother's hysterectomy.

At the end of the first week, the girls lined up to exchange linens. She had stood in line with the bottom sheet to turn in along with her towels.

"Here's mine," she had said, handing the pile to her counselor, Gretchen.

"Where's the other sheet?"

"On the bed." She had already carefully tucked last week's top sheet into the bottom sheet position. It had taken quite a while to get the envelope corners tight as Gretchen had prescribed.

"You get two clean sheets each week."

Sharon expected Gretchen to get mad now with the discovery that she wasn't following the rules. But instead, Gretchen had put her arm around her and explained carefully while the other girls listened and poked each other that here at camp they would get two clean sheets and two clean towels. There was plenty of clean laundry for everyone.

Thirty years later, Sharon still felt humiliated. How was she supposed to have known that not everyone changed only one sheet per week? Her mother's device of moving the top sheet to the bottom for a second week was just another of her embarrassing habits of thrift. She should now find this recollection amusing, but it wasn't and instead reinforced her sense of the need to do most of the talking at Shady Grove.

They pulled up under the awning in front, just behind a turquoise bus splashed with "Fun Bus—The Go-Getters at

Shady Grove." Sharon let the car idle, regretting this timing. Betty rolled down her window to get a better view. The driver got out, opened the side door, and let down the wheelchair ramp. An attendant from the bus unclamped the latches that held a wheelchair in place inside the van, rolled it onto the ramp, re-clamped it there, and then pushed a lever that lowered the ramp. The wheelchair arrived at ground level grandly, like the Pope, Betty thought. Another attendant, a woman in scrubs printed with clowns, unclamped the chair and pushed it toward the entrance.

"There you go, doll," she leaned over to shout to a woman slumped into blankets like a turtle. "Didn't we enjoy that shopping?"

Betty could tell Sharon didn't want her to watch too closely because Sharon closed the window with her own controls. Finally, four passengers climbed out on their own steam carrying shopping bags. The wheelchair lady was met by a teenaged employee and rolled quickly away. Finally, Sharon was able to park, and Betty hurried to get out before anyone could assist her. Together, they went through a double door and under an elaborate brass chandelier loaded with candle bulbs in a carpeted lobby.

Betty was treated like a queen in the reception office—Coffee? Juice? Water?—while they waited for Monique to be ready for them. Betty looked at the paintings that featured country vistas and sunsets with furry animals involved in some way. Sharon chatted with the receptionist.

Finally, Monique greeted them, pressing and holding Betty's hand. "Mrs. Miles, how nice of you to visit with us."

Monique was wearing what Betty called a Mother Hubbard dress, a long linen affair that brushed her ankles.

It reminded Betty of what her mother had worn for laundry day. She thought about their Mondays in the basement with the Maytag electric wringer. How her mother had loved that washing machine, "such a convenience," she had said.

"Keep your mind on your business. Watch your fingers, Bet!" As the middle daughter, her job was feeding the flour bag dish towels, her father's long johns, and her mother's slips or housedresses into the rollers that squeezed the cotton into long tongues that poked out the other side and drooped into the waiting baskets. In winter, they hung up the laundry by the furnace. By the end of the morning, the basement was warm and moist like a July day. When her mother was upstairs, she would open the furnace door just to look inside at the coals glowing like hell itself.

A jingling brought Betty back with a jerk to the small office where Monique was still gripping her hand. Betty realized that the sound was the tinkle of Monique's bracelet, rows of tiny giraffes linked by tangles of chains.

"It's a special day here, Betty. We hope you'll join us for lunch. The Sunshine Chorus will be performing at noon."

"I'm not sure we can stay that long."

Monique smiled at Sharon and patted Betty's hand, saying, "Oh, I hope you can, Betty."

We're already on a first-name basis! But this was the way service people used your first name to put you in your place, lest you think of making a complaint.

The reception door opened and a man stepped in, perhaps in his early eighties, athletic, in a tracksuit, and only slightly stooped.

Monique appeared delighted. "Here's Paul now to show us around." She spoke loudly. "Paul, this is Betty Miles and her daughter Sharon." He bowed. "Paul will give you all the details."

"Pleased to meet you. Now which one is the daughter?" He scratched his head.

Betty laughed to show Sharon what a good sport she was.

"Well, girls, let's put the pedal to the metal and get going." He extended one arm to each woman. Though Betty drew back, Monique guided her into position, and they headed out under the chandelier. Paul ducked his head.

"Always want to duck going under that monstrosity. Builders, they think all old people are short." He swung them around square-dance style to face the dining room. Betty took a better grip on his arm.

"Our dining establishment—two meals a day. Breakfast is on your own, like they say on a European tour. More of those low flying aircraft, but at least here you're sitting down." Paul gestured to mini-versions of the chandeliers that hung here and there.

Sharon asked Paul how long he'd been living here. "Four years, ever since my wife passed. I moved here before my son and his wife got too bossy." Sharon's smile faded.

They made a few turns down windowless corridors, passing an entertainment room, chapel, game room, and library. It made Betty think of a navy ship she had once toured. In fact, the building even seemed to lurch as she looked down the long hall, and the association became even stronger as she noted that handrails ran along the corridors. She took an even firmer grip on Paul's arm and felt a slight squeeze in return.

They paused in front of the exercise room. "The Merry Widows," Paul said, gesturing toward the half dozen women in Popsicle-colored nylon suits bicycling calmly. "The hubby is hardly cold and another member joins the group. Going to the malls, dinner, shows, you name it. Guess there's a lesson there." Paul shook his head.

Betty thought about Charlie. She had found him in his lounge chair, a bit blue but peaceful looking. In his hand had been the TV remote. A small dam had burst in her at that terrible moment, surprise, regret, and relief flowing out in equal parts. The loneliness had come after, of course, but it had been bearable.

"Can we see a typical apartment, Paul?" Sharon interrupted her thoughts, though Betty noticed Sharon too seemed transfixed by the Merry Widows.

"I'm going to show you mine."

They swept down an intersecting corridor, where again Betty noticed railings for rough weather, it seemed. Since each section of the building had a name—Misty Glen, Deer Valley, Autumn Lane—walking through the halls was a trip in itself. Would they cross Alligator Hole? Betty wondered. In Spring Breeze, Paul flung open a door. The mini-kitchen, living room, bedroom, and bath were on view the minute the door opened. No hiding any contraband in here, Betty thought. Since Paul was on the first floor, his quarters had a patio door leading out to a square of concrete with potted geraniums.

"You've got to step outside to change your mind, but everything's convenient." He opened the closet and a cupboard or two that seemed rather empty.

Betty and Sharon murmured a few compliments while Sharon thought about how the whole place was hardly larger than her den. She would bet dollars-to-doughnuts that Monique would never recommend Shady Grove to any of her own family members, and if she did, they would immediately reject the whole idea.

Betty paused by the patio door again. Her duplex had only a small front porch, too limited even for a good chair. Here, she could set out two or three chairs. The inside, however, was too small for all her living room furniture. The electric chair would have to go.

When they made their way back to the reception area, Betty watched Monique engineer a few minutes alone with Sharon by suggesting Paul go over the activities schedule. He drew Betty to a wall calendar decorated with stickers. She had never been a joiner other than cards occasionally. Her interests were more solitary like reading or handiwork. In large print, the chart announced the daily events, such as a plant party, kitchen magicians, origami, a grocery outing, and, mysteriously, swinging singles.

Feeling she should say something, Betty said, "Well."

"It's not so bad, really." Paul smiled. "Best part is I can say *no* to my son's wife."

"Did you live with them?"

"For about three months, but my daughter-in-law's an organizer."

"I know what you mean," Betty said, thinking of the electric chair.

"'Paul, you should take these vitamins. . . . Paul, you know you should eat more vegetables.'" He lowered his voice: "Then she got to asking . . . '*Paul, have you made a jobbie yet today?*' I figured I'd had enough."

"Well, really, I think I'd better find the lobby." Betty drew away.

"So, since I'm here like they wanted, what more can they ask? As I see it, my debt is paid," Paul concluded. "Something else I like here is boundaries. When my wife died, that's what I missed the most. I could have Wheaties for dinner, watch TV all night, and do whatever whenever, but that kind of freedom didn't make me feel any better. Here, it's lunch eleven thirty to one, cocktails at four, dinner from five to six thirty. Keeps me grounded."

Betty nodded. He did have a point. After Charlie passed away, she tossed and turned in bed, having gotten ready either too early or too late because she had nibbled instead of making dinner on time or forgotten about it altogether.

After they made their way back along the confusing halls, she gazed around at the front lobby and dayroom. Though the whole place was supposed to make you feel like you were on permanent vacation, she wasn't sure the cruise ship was headed any place she wanted to go.

Paul put his arm on her shoulder. "You should move here, Betty. It'll be all right, and it will please your daughter. That's worth a lot."

When Sharon came out, Monique invited Betty into her office, leaving Sharon with the receptionist. She offered coffee or juice again. Betty declined and sat down across from the sunset picture.

"Mrs. Miles," for some reason Monique had gone back to her last name, "I'd like to describe our health services. First of all, do you have any questions?"

"Yes," said Betty. "Where do I sign?"

"Excuse me?" Her giraffes jingled in alarm.

Betty felt a small thrill getting a step ahead of this manipulative young woman. "Where do I sign to get an apartment? I'd like one on the first floor, like Paul's." She paused. "In fact, I'd like that one you expect to be—how did you put it—*available* soon that's right near him."

"Let's just look over the Resident's Bill of Rights, shall we, Betty?" Monique was about to sit next to her on the sofa.

"*Monique*," it felt so good to address her this way, "Paul said he was a retired attorney. If whatever is in there is good enough for him, I'm satisfied." Betty opened her purse to get a pen. She felt that the ball was in her court and searched for a more unreasonable request to make.

"Something else, Monique."

"Yes?"

"I am thinking of getting a pet, something small to care for. They say it makes you live longer, you know." She glanced pointedly at Monique's bracelet.

"Yes, so I've heard. What kind of pet do you have in mind?"

Betty felt a bubble of hilarity rising. "An amphibian." She watched Monique try to think of species examples to prepare an answer and then went on, "Let's get this paperwork ready for me to sign." She snapped her purse shut.

They agreed that Monique would send a representative over later in the week with the completed agreements. Betty could move in as soon as the apartment was available and repainted. Taking a cue from Judge Judy, Betty decided to have the last word on her way out.

"You know this place could use some new artwork." She picked up her purse and marched out before Monique, the receptionist, or Sharon could take her arm.

When they were back in the car, Betty said, "Well, it's all settled."

So this was a refusal to look at any senior apartments ever, Sharon thought. "Mother, you should at least give it some thought."

Her hands tightened on the wheel. Here was her day off half over and nothing accomplished, just typical of trying to get her mother to make a decision now that her father was gone. He had made most of the decisions about their lives—didn't she remember that well!

"I have thought about it."

Betty noticed how Sharon's right eye still squinted ever so slightly when she wasn't about to give up on something. How many times had Betty told her she couldn't have a horse, and yet she still asked and asked: "Just think about it, *please*," she would say quietly, her eye giving a twitch.

Betty's elation over her surprise was deflating, so she delivered her news in one blow. "As soon as an apartment becomes available, I'll be moving to Shady Grove, dear. I signed up today."

"Today?" Sharon pulled the car over. Was her mother having some kind of attack? Was she quite all right?

"Yes, they're sending a lawyer over Thursday so I can sign the remaining paperwork. Monique said she would help me pick out what furniture to bring. I don't want to be a nuisance anymore to you and Vince."

Nuisance zeroed in on Sharon like a smart bomb.

Yes, it was a nuisance to have her mother on her mind all the time. Well, nuisance wasn't quite the right word. Inconvenience? More like anxiety. Her health, her appointments, her banking, and so forth.

She was lucky to have her mother, she knew. Other women had lost theirs much sooner and reminded Sharon often of her good fortune. But now that her mother had agreed to this next life stage, she wasn't sure she approved. What would it be like not to call her mother each morning at nine and drop in at the duplex if she sounded "off"? How would someone else learn what kind of library books she wanted or which sweater was dry-clean only? Would Monique be the one she talked to now about *Jeopardy*? Who would daily make Sharon feel like Lady Bountiful?

Maybe Vince had been right about the wait and see.

5

Liberation

As the realtor had predicted, the duplex sold very quickly. Sharon had insisted on cleaning at least twice a week and Betty gave in, simply sitting on the couch while Sharon poked the vacuum cleaner into corners and arranged the fresh flowers she brought for the dinette table. Within two weeks, a brother and sister bought it planning to move in their father.

Sharon was puzzled that even the sale of her extra furniture seemed to leave her mother unflappable in her preparations to move to Shady Grove. Betty had put an ad in the paper to sell a few antiques that Sharon didn't want and missed them for only a few minutes after their departure. She sold her collection of salt-and-peppershakers to a dealer from New York, saving only three of her favorites—Jack and Jill, the red tomatoes, and the Michigan lighthouses—and gave a set of mother hen and chicks to Sharon. Then she moved with steamroller determination through her cupboards, setting out for the resale shop canning equipment, plasticware, soufflé dishes, salad molds, novelty cake pans, and even a set of everyday cutlery.

"If I don't use my sterling now, I never will," Betty said, vowing she would use it for her breakfasts at Shady Grove, since the other meals she would eat in the dining room. She could picture the wedding flatware laid on some nice tablecloths on the dinette table, which she planned to put in front of the door to her east-facing patio. A drawback of the duplex, no sunshine had reached her table. From now on at breakfast, she would set out her mother's tea set and eat on the sterling. Yes, she would live like Mrs. GotRocks.

Next, she went through her just-in-case items like spot remover, starch, a plunger, mineral spirits, and extension cords. The pile grew bigger in her garage, which was unused since selling her car after a minor accident. Next, she hit the closets, setting out umbrellas, boots, and a snow shovel, as well as embroidered card table covers, bedspreads, and guest linens that dated back to her hope chest. Finally, some of the memorabilia went, even the colonial candlesticks Sharon and Vince had picked out for her on their trip to Williamsburg just last year.

This ambitious cleanout made Sharon feel worse and worse. Why, her mother was doing the kind of disposal you had to do for the dead. Was this her mother's way of getting back at her for suggesting Shady Grove—disposing bit by bit of herself and daughter too, for that matter, since familiar items of her childhood were now headed to strangers or the landfill?

Finally, Sharon put her foot down when Betty began tossing Christmas decorations into the trash. "Mother, you will need some of these things. There will be Christmas at Shady Grove too, you know."

Betty did know this. She could already picture how done to death Christmas would be there. On top of the commercially prepared decorations at every turn there would be paper chains, Santa Clauses, snowflakes, and reindeer contributed by Scouts, Sunday schoolers, and others looking for a way to escape the commercialism and meaninglessness of the holiday season by giving to others.

Instead of being depressed, Betty felt liberated. Of course, she had already parted with much of her furniture in moving to the duplex. But in moving there she had taken most of her old life and routine with her, just crammed it into smaller quarters. Things would be different from now on.

"I just want to keep things simple and elegant when I get there," she said.

Since moving the burden of her care from Sharon to others was her goal, cleaning out a lot of stuff made sense to Betty. She was so busy with her cleaning that she had to forego some of her morning television. Those chatty news anchors would have to get along without an invitation to her kitchen some mornings. Going through her cookbook collection and her boxes of letters took too much concentration to have background noise. This part of her cleanout was inescapably depressing—many boxes put away very carefully—her mother's address book, family greeting cards, and random party photos that Charlie had taken; she rarely if ever got these things out to look at. Betty wondered if her memory would preserve these moments after the objects were gone. And these memories would surely be gone after she was.

Her final day in the duplex came just a month after writing her check for the first three months at Shady Grove. A few boxes remained, and she had saved these for her last day, because these were boxes of mementos from Sharon's childhood. Even so many years later, she couldn't bear to throw out these things, but truly there was not room in the new apartment. Here was the bunny sweater she had gotten Sharon one Easter, a pair of pink ballet shoes, and her Girl Scout uniform with many badges on a sash. Sharon had worked very hard on all badges related to cooking—cake decorating, campfire cookery, edible plants, and even home canning. Betty and Charlie had eaten many highlights and disasters to show their own appreciation. Betty supposed her business of demonstrating and selling high-priced kitchen gadgets dated to this early interest. Oh, wait, Sharon called this stuff *high-end utensils*.

Betty set aside the sweater along with letters and Mother's Day cards but put the Scout uniform back in a box. Finally, she stuffed Sharon's old school papers and report cards in a large envelope. What did these signify anymore, especially the report card stating Sharon was sometimes impatient with her classmates? If Sharon didn't want these, they would go to the trash, but the bunny sweater and the cards, well, she would bring them along to Shady Grove, no matter what.

With that decision made and the sweater and cards tucked in a drawer, Betty was ready for a nap and was about to get the timer, then remembered that it had already been packed.

"I don't need it anyway," she addressed Charlie's picture. She settled in her favorite chair that remained along with its pal, the electric chair, and tipped her head back.

She drifted off.

It seemed to her that she was lying at the bottom of some stairs looking up. She tried to move and couldn't. "Agh, agh."

Who would hear her down here? Her breathing became quick and light. She could die right here and no one would find her. She had gone down these stairs looking for something.

Bang. Bang, bang!

Betty tried again to make a sound to attract attention. "Heeelp!" This vocal effort jerked her awake.

She was sitting in her chair with her feet firmly on the floor, but the banging continued. Oh no, it was Stanislav Pularski. Had her calls for help brought him right to her window?

There he was in his bathrobe with its loose cord. She knew all about that. When she had first moved in, he had come over asking to use her phone. The poor man had been locked out in his bathrobe while getting his newspaper off the lawn. He had seemed dangerously out of breath when he appeared at her door. Betty knew her short-term memory was unreliable but not concerning Stanislav.

"Come right in and sit down," she had said. Well, soon enough she discovered it wasn't being locked out that was his problem. When he yanked the bathrobe cord, she saw enough of Stanislav to last a lifetime. Goodness, and here he was again, his face plastered to her window, here to save her. She thought about Mary Grace's neighbor waiting for the funeral home director. That might be better.

"I'm fine, Stan. I'm fine. You go home now." Betty put her face near the window and pointed toward his duplex. He stood there a moment longer and gave up. How many Stanislavs would there be at Shady Grove? Betty wondered.

About five thirty, Vince came by and picked up a few boxes to store in their attic—some glassware and a set of china too nice for the yard sale and maybe the scout uniform, Betty hoped.

"Whatcha watching, Mom?"

"Oh, just whatever's on."

Actually, it was one of her favorites—truckers of the icy trans-Alaskan highway. The tension caused by the weather was exciting, especially with a woman driver behind the wheel. The dark and cold up there, the snow, and the northern lights! Just imagine! She watched every episode.

Unlike Sharon, who had said before that Betty's taste was perverse, Vince sat down in the electric chair immediately. Betty found some peanuts, and they followed the competing truckers. Betty cried, "You go, girl!" as their favorite gal performed a roadside repair in a blizzard. When she skidded ahead of schedule into the next truckstop, Vince pumped his fist. Then he reminisced about his drive along the same route one summer in high school.

"Your parents let you go so far away?"

"Well, my brother and I were supposed to be driving to Seattle to see an uncle. We didn't mention we were going the long way around!"

"Good for you. Your parents had a fit when they found out?"

"Took my driver's license away for three months!" He and Betty laughed.

Getting up to leave, he sighed. They had had some good times in this duplex. Sometimes he had made chili, while his mother-in-law popped corn, never complaining about his menu choices.

"Got to go, Mom. Sharon and I'll be along in the morning with the panel truck."

Betty walked him to the door, also feeling sentimental all of a sudden about leaving the next day.

"Thanks for everything, Vince. What would I do without you?" He had been so helpful, and she thought he looked rather hangdog lately.

He gave her a peck on the cheek. No one could ask for a better son-in-law, she thought, and watched his taillights recede as he turned from her cul-de-sac. *Funny that he turned right, not left toward his house.* Must be he was on an errand for Sharon before going home. She watched the news and went to bed early, chilly under the single blanket that was left.

In the morning for breakfast, Betty set out the little bit that was left in the fridge, a slice of cheese and some applesauce, thinking how quickly the four years she had been here had passed. Why was it that when you got older the time seemed to race, even though from moment to moment time seemed to hang heavy on your hands? It was a puzzle.

She took her plate to the table and looked around the nearly empty room, musing about all her homes now that she was moving on to what would surely be her final one. First had been the grey clapboard farmhouse where she was born, the second of the sisters, all gone now except for her. Down the road each way were other farm families. Each had sons, big, hulking boys who talked only about "huntin' 'n fishin'" and dropped out of school as soon as possible. Modern people thought growing up on a farm to be wholesome, but the truth was that it was dirty and boring. The men were coarse, and with big families, big gardens, and farm animals to deal with, the women were just about worked to death.

Betty made getting away from the farm her primary occupation after graduation. While working in town, she had met Charlie, an affable newcomer. They married after a suitably long engagement, and they moved to town to a brick bungalow on Wood Street. Betty felt that with Charlie to keep her company the days seemed full of possibilities, even when his awful mother came over on Sundays. Then finally along came Sharon. All her needs seemed fulfilled forever while holding her pretty baby in her arms.

Betty turned to Charlie's photo, which was now on the kitchen counter—it just hadn't felt right to bury him in a packing box even for a few days.

"Seventy-five dollars we paid on our mortgage each month. Your mother said it was sinful to spend when we could live with her. But I still think I was right that we should have our own place, don't you?"

As usual, he agreed, his lip curling, eyebrow rising, ready to give her one of his million-dollar smiles, the smiles that sold so much insurance.

6
Late Night Rendezvous

*E*arly the next morning, Sharon and Vince cleaned out his panel van so that there would be plenty of room for Betty's things, but with as much as they had sold, it wouldn't take even two trips. Sharon had orchestrated this departure from the duplex carefully. A scene with crying and recriminations would be too awful. They made final plans as they turned the corner to Betty's street.

"Vince, back right into the driveway so we can open the back van doors. You know how mother hates to make a spectacle of herself," Sharon said as they neared the duplex. She noticed the drapes were still drawn—a sign of her mother's mood? She hoped not.

Vince obediently backed in, leaving just enough room for the doors to swing open. He knew it was Sharon who wanted privacy. Getting her mother to make this move had been hard on his wife. He understood her worry about her mother's being alone and the professional failure she felt at being unable to make up her own mind, or her mother's, about the rightness of going to Shady Grove rather than inviting her to their house to live.

"I'll let myself in, and we'll let her help carry some of the stuff out, just to make her feel empowered." Vince rolled his eyes, but not so Sharon could see.

"Okay, I'll put the big stuff in first. Open the garage, would you?"

When Sharon pressed in the code outside, the door arose to reveal Betty as if on stage, sitting on the edge of an end table in her coat and carrying her navy purse.

"Mother, have you been sitting out here very long? Why are you out here?"

"I have everything ready to go indoors and the refrigerator is empty. I was going to turn off the power, but you wouldn't be able to get in the garage."

"You don't need to turn off the power." This was so like her mother, probably thinking someone would be mad at her for leaving the power on.

Sharon looked her over carefully. Yes, she had on her new green slacks—that was a good sign—but Sharon herself felt a hint of depression, then self-disgust: Why should she feel bad that her mother appeared to feel good about moving to assisted living?

"Here, Mom, why don't you sit in the van while Vince and I load it."

"Whatever you say, honey." Betty took Sharon's arm and used the step stool to reach the bench seat in the front. She watched as they loaded in the boxes and her furniture.

"That girl should look happier," Betty said, "now that she won't have to worry about me any longer."

—〰—

Even though it was Saturday, Monique was on hand when Sharon and Betty came in the lobby. It had taken only an hour to fill the van, turn over the keys to the realtor, and drive to Shady Grove.

"Betty, welcome, welcome to our community!" Monique's bracelets mashed into Betty's wrists as she took each of Betty's arms in a hug.

Betty noted that she wasn't *Mrs. Miles* anymore, just a one-name inmate, or no, *community member*. When Monique offered to take her purse and coat, Betty only let go of her coat. In the spirit of the photos in the senior living brochure, Betty had worn a new cotton polo shirt with a botanical print of spring flowers and her green slacks. Though she wanted to pitch in on the unpacking, it wasn't too soon to turn over the new leaf of living with style. Sharon and Vince looked like the cleaning crew in their I-heart-Indiana sweatshirts, but Betty knew Sharon had some nice sweaters for visiting or events at Shady Grove. Monique led them to the apartment and flung open the door grandly. The three rooms had been repainted—the same beige as before, except for the bathroom, which was now blue—and the gold carpet had been steamed. The miniature refrigerator and microwave were brand new, as Sharon had insisted.

A couple of maintenance men helped Vince with Betty's bed, dresser, and small desk for the bedroom, and for the living room/kitchen/eating area, her favorite blue chair, TV, a bookcase to set the TV on, and the electric chair, which she had marked for the Salvation Army and Sharon had rescued. The dinette table with its four chairs still sat in the corridor.

"The table should go right here," Monique directed Vince. He maneuvered it through the door and placed it in the eating area. Then it was impossible to open the kitchen cabinet's lower doors.

Monique frowned. "Sharon, you may want to get Mom a table for one."

"Actually," Betty stepped to her Hepplewhite dinette table, "Vince, I'd like my table in front of my patio door." She wouldn't let this officious babe (or the other b-word) make all the decisions.

By moving the electric chair, they found a place for the table and chairs in front of the window. Sharon suggested the desk would work well along the eating area wall. It troubled her there was so little counter space, but the facility had a kitchen/craft/plant room for residents who wanted to bake. Perhaps she would volunteer to lead some sessions. That might be fun and give her time with her mother.

During the afternoon, a parade of people interrupted their unpacking—the facility director, the case manager, the nurse, the activities director, two housekeeping personnel, and two aides all welcomed the family with genuine warmth. It will be a job to keep all these helpers straight, Betty thought. Sharon greeted each with enthusiasm, articulating again the role each would play in her mother's new home.

Betty was gratified to see her daughter now acting so pleased with all the arrangements. The two of them sorted through boxes and unpacked her good dishes, arranging a few teacups and her remaining salt-and-peppershakers along the counter.

"Look, Mother, what nice shelves you have for towels and sheets. Your last place didn't have a linen closet."

"Yes, you're right, honey. Everything is perfect."

The sunflower rug would have looked nice by the linen closet, but it was at a resale shop now. Oh well, she could catch the Shady Grove bus for a shopping trip to find another one (or perhaps retrieve the same one). And maybe some new towels too. It would be fun to have everything just so in this dollhouse.

Supper—it was called *supper* at Shady Grove—passed in a confusing delivery of instructions and introductions.

"Since most folks like their hot meal at noon, dinner is sandwiches," the dining hostess explained.

Vince felt dispirited over the choice of turkey or ham sandwiches that looked rather downscale on a buffet table under three chandeliers. There was also a kettle of chicken soup and several desserts with white foam on top. "Did they make these at noon before the cooks left?" he muttered. Sharon shushed him and guided them to the table where Betty had an assigned seat.

Monique stood and tapped a glass with a spoon. "I'd like us all to give Betty Miles our official welcome to our community at Shady Grove."

She helped Betty stand up and Paul led the group in a quiet applause, though many smiled warmly. A couple Betty knew from her old neighborhood offered to show her around the next day. An energetic woman invited her to the yoga class. After supper, Sharon, Vince, and Betty refused an offer to watch a movie in the entertainment center and went back to the apartment.

"You go on home now. It's time for me to settle in, dear. Thanks for everything, Vince."

"You'll be okay, Mother? Want me to stay the night, your first night?"

Out of nowhere, Sharon felt a wash of loneliness like her first night at camp when her parents left her. She had begged them to sleep in their car in the parking lot, she recalled. Well, she could do better than that for her mother. She could stay here for the night in the recliner chair.

"Of course not. I'll be snug as a bug in a rug." Betty put her arm around Sharon and held up her jacket.

"Yup, I think they cleaned the rugs," Vince said. "Come on, honey."

Finally, they backed out the door after one more hug. Betty recalled her tearful Sharon her first time at sleep-away camp. She and Charlie had felt terrible leaving her so miserable. Did Sharon still remember that at all? Probably not.

After the door closed on her family, Betty, as well as her things it seemed, breathed a sigh of relief. She toured her new digs slowly. Her table in front of the window gave her place a different look from the standard she'd seen through other open doors: couch on the north wall, television on the south wall, coffee table center, *Reader's Digest* and the AARP magazine centered on the table, and dinky breakfast table by the bathroom door. Now it was time to arrange the family photos.

Charlie had spent the last few hours packed in her lingerie drawer for safety. She giggled. "Hope you had fun in there!" Yes, in the old days, he had complained about flannel.

Where to put him here? It was her favorite photo of him, taken about twenty years ago to use for sales brochures and newsletters. She liked the star panache the black and white photo seemed to impart. He had been a handsome man with a full head of silver hair.

"Well, Chipper, you escaped assisted living, but I haven't. Let me show you around." He seemed agreeable, his lips in an almost-smile.

"The living room. See, I put your favorite photo of your darling girl on the bookcase." She held the photos face-to-face.

"The bedroom. Yes, I've still got our double bed. The room's kind of small for it though."

"The ba-a-a-th." She whooshed the door open. "Look at this shower that's like a walk-in bathtub!"

She returned to the living room. "I'm going to put you right here on the end of the bookcase, so you can see everyone coming and going." He maintained his pleasant expression. Whether he would have agreed to move here as a couple, she wasn't sure.

Betty had just taken off her slacks when someone knocked on the door. Goodness, the hall door was awfully close to where she was standing bare legged in her bedroom.

"Betty?" Another knock. "Betty!"

"Just a minute." Someone was nervy enough to try to turn the knob. Since her bathrobe was still folded up, she grabbed her coat off the bed.

"Yes?" She inched the door partway open to find Monique, who looked her up and down.

"Betty, I came to see if you're going to take a shower or bath tonight." She was holding a clipboard.

"No, not now."

"If you'll just let me know when, I'll send an aide to help out. Tomorrow a.m.? Seven thirty?"

"I'm sure I can do it alone, thank you." She pulled her coat closed more securely.

Monique stared pointedly at her coat. "Ah, Betty, when residents go out of the community, they must sign out. Just so we know where—"

"I'm not going out now. I'm going to bed." No doubt, she would be marked on the clipboard as *deranged,* like the woman at the public library who wore a parka winter and summer.

"Always remember help is just a few feet away." Something that was quite evident from the sounds of other people's radios and televisions and the clank of a medication cart.

"Here let me remind you where the help call buttons are." Monique pushed past her. Yes, she knew they were in the bathroom and bedroom on long white cords that made her think of an old-fashioned douche hose. Vince had clowned around earlier, pretending to hang himself.

"Why don't I just send Sandy in to help you get ready for bed, Betty?" Monique was eyeing her coat and bare feet.

"That won't be necessary." Didn't this woman have her own home where she could bother people? "I was unpacking my nightdress and robe when you knocked. Good night."

Finally, Monique departed. Unlike her duplex or a hotel room, this unit did not have a chain for the door. After wiggling into her nightgown, she gave Charlie and Sharon their usual kisses before working her way through the unfamiliar light switches. Thankfully, her bed felt so familiar, she quickly fell asleep about eleven, and as usual about two thirty, nature called. She went into the bathroom where the chunky toilet seat, which seemed to rise up to meet her bottom, nearly tipped her over, a reminder she wasn't at home. *No, she was in her new home with appliances for the golden years.*

Now fully awake, she settled into her favorite chair and took in her new nighttime environment that certainly had an institutional undertone—someone passed by in the hall pushing a floor polisher leaving a scent of official clean and a phone rang somewhere. Yes, these sounds were evidence of nearby help for a stroke, heart attack, lost dentures, or whatever else might come. She looked toward her patio.

A man was standing out there! That help buzzer might come in handy on her first night. But, no, it was neighbor Paul. Poor Paul! He must be confused, sun-downing, it was called, such a pretty name for the dementia that impelled you to wander at night searching for *home.* No wonder his daughter-in-law put him here in assisted living! He had seemed alert at dinner, stopping to chat with them and swiping the dinner table daisies to present as a welcome gift. Well, no point in ringing the buzzer, she would shoo him along to his own apartment or walk him to the attendant's station.

Betty opened her patio door just as he turned and waved, no, blew a kiss, to someone else standing outside. Why, it was the very well-endowed woman who lived two units over. On the buffet line at supper, her bazoombas (there was no other word for them) were so exposed and shelf-like, Vince had difficulty reaching the soup ladle. Betty watched

her gesture of catching the kiss and placing it by her ear-
lobe. Of course.

As he sidled like a cat burglar across her patio, Paul
didn't notice Betty in her nightgown, the lady to whom he
had presented daisies just a few hours before. She locked
her patio door, rechecked the hall door, and went back to
bed.

Months later when Betty thought over her first week, the
memories seemed like vacation postcards about acclimat-
ing to a foreign port. Local customs, entertainment, and
policing of the indigenous peoples required much study. For
the first few days, staff members tapped on her door nearly
hourly inviting her to an activity. Their disappointment was
so obvious if she declined that Betty usually agreed. To go
native, she joined the kitchen band by strumming a cheese
grater with a wooden spoon to "Oh, Suzanna"; she made a
bird feeder in arts and crafts, did chair-side exercise, and
attended a production by the Clip Clop Cloggers, golden-
agers who performed at schools and the county fair. Perhaps
living at Shady Grove would turn out to be "a hoot."

One afternoon when she was lingering out on the front
porch, Mabel, in her swaying Pontiac, pulled up. "Come on!
Let's go to the resale shops, Betty."

"Oh, that would be a relief from all the fun here," Betty
laughed and recounted how she had helped with napkin
folding for the dining room that morning. "The first useful
thing I've done in a week!"

By the time they visited three shops—Betty found a Dior hat at the Episcopalian shop—two hours had passed. On her way back through the lobby, Betty saw Monique motion for her to come into her office.

"Step in, please, Betty." *Now what?* Betty wondered.

"You have been out?" Today Monique wore a heavy necklace with a silver medallion engraved with a tiger. The woman had a menagerie trapped in her jewelry box.

"Oh, yes, my friend picked me up, and we went to the resale shops."

"Community members are supposed to sign out if they leave the campus."

"I'm sorry. I forgot." Betty caught herself before she actually hung her head. Good grief! This wasn't the principal's office.

"Yes, right here you should put your name, the time, and where you are going. And preferably, someone—your daughter, for example—signs you out." She pointed to a little pile of forms. "And . . . next time you could consider going to the secondhand shops with our group on, let's see, the third Tuesday. That way an aide will be nearby in case of, well, just in case."

"I see."

What more was there to say? Betty marched back along the corridors to her quarters after her encounter with community policing. So larking around with Mabel at the drop of a hat was off limits. At least Sharon would be pleased.

—⚬⚬⚬—

By the end of the second week, Betty could hold off her bridge girls no longer. They longed to see her new situation, so she suggested they hold their weekly card session at Shady Grove. They would tour her apartment first and then play bridge in the formal dayroom that had cherry-finished furniture, a large flat-screen television, a piano, and even a grandfather clock. Carpet and drapes were a green and pink floral; the whole effect was dressy, like a parlor in a posh funeral home, Betty thought. They would use the cherry-finished card table with the brocade (slightly stained) chairs and could serve themselves coffee from the corner hutch.

Monique brought Ardyce, Irene, and Bernice to Betty's apartment after detouring them though her office for brochures. "Betty has fit in very well to our community already," she assured them and left reluctantly, it seemed to Betty.

Her friends examined every inch of the new quarters.

"Very cute, Betty," said Bernice. "I'll crochet you a new tissue box cover to go with your new bathroom." The last one shaped like a top hat had gone in the yard sale.

Ardyce thought the cupboards were pressed wood, not like the birch cabinets her son had in mind for her.

Irene congratulated her on getting a unit with a patio door to the outside. "That will be very nice in the good weather. You can add some deck furniture." She had put down extra money to have a golf course walkout in the senior living place being built in Florida, she reminded them.

As they walked toward the dayroom, Betty couldn't resist telling them about the goings-on she had already observed out the patio door.

Ardyce looked around for eavesdroppers. "Well, remember what that lady doctor said at the senior center health fair?"

Betty did not.

"She said places like this," Ardyce gestured inclusive of the surroundings, "are awash with chlamydia and other things like it. I certainly wouldn't use that bathroom," she tipped her head toward an extra wide door, "if I were you."

"Oh, for heaven's sake! This looks like a lovely facility. Don't be so critical." It was nice of Irene to stick up for her, but Betty noticed she didn't say *lovely home* or even *complex*.

They enjoyed bridge in the dayroom with only a few distractions. An elderly man and his family carried on a loud conversation:

"Do you like it here, Dad?"

"What?"

"Do they feed you good, Dad?"

"Where's my mail?"

"We'll take care of your mail. You take it easy."

"Who's paying for this?"

Later, Paul came by. "Hello, neighbor," he bowed to Betty. "Cards today, I see." He had on a red workout jacket and pants.

Betty introduced her friends, and though Irene offered to sit out a hand so he could play, he declined but gave Betty's shoulder a squeeze as he thanked them.

"Is he the one?" Bernice whispered.

"Yes, apparently he's quite the Casanova." Betty thought he looked silly in the red outfit.

"You could do worse, Betty."

"I'm not interested in men!" Even to herself, her declaration sounded like a jilted teen.

Their card party wound up at four, and the friends made their way around several residents in wheelchairs parked near the dining room. Irene squeezed the hand of a woman who reached for her as she passed. Ardyce whispered that these people should be kept in the other wing, and Bernice assured Betty that she would like it here, eventually.

"Thanks so much for hosting, Betty, but how about next week we meet at the senior center, as usual?" An idea endorsed by all.

Monique came out of her office too late to wish them goodbye.

Betty was pleased by Sharon's interest in how well she was *adjusting to* Shady Grove. In fact, Sharon still called her nearly every day. Betty regaled her with Paul's late night-rendezvous and described her interest in the computer class. At last, she might do e-mail. Or even Facebook, and—what was it called?—make a profile.

"Facebook, Mom? Really? Are you going to look for old friends?"

"Most people seem to keep track of their grandchildren on Facebook." Oh, that was the wrong thing to say to Sharon.

"Well, I'd like to look at the w-w-w pages too, of course. You have a w-w-w page for your business, don't you?"

"I've showed you my website a lot of times."

Betty sensed the need to change the subject, so she described the morning bingo sessions at nine when vocational students came in to call the numbers.

During another phone conversation, Betty had news about a bridge tournament. "Oh, honey, guess what. You remember the Helms down at the Elks? My partner and I here beat the pants off them yesterday!"

"Good for you. I always felt sorry for their daughter. Her father told her the Beatles were Communists, and she wasn't allowed to listen to a single song."

"That does sound like Murf. He's not saying anything much now since he's had a stroke, but he still plays bridge like a shark." In the old days, Murf had given her the eye a few times, but she had set him straight right away.

"So, everything is all right, Mom?" Betty got the drift of the question.

"Yes, dear, quite a lively bunch here. It's really a hoot."

Sharon was sitting at her desk with her calendar, simultaneously listening to her mother and figuring her demonstration party schedule. Had she heard correctly? A *hoot*? Now what did that mean? Why couldn't her mother come right out and say what she meant? Was she liking it at Shady Grove, or not?

Betty hastened to fill the silence. "Please tell Vince I won't need a ride to the NuLook on Monday."

"You're not getting your hair done?"

"Oh, then I'd be a fright! No, instead of going out, I'll have it done right here. That reminds me, you don't need to take me to the library either."

That freed up Thursday lunch hour on her schedule, Sharon noted, but she hesitated before deleting, "Mother."

"Mom, I can still take you to the library." It was a small thing, after all, just during her lunch break.

"Oh, we have one here, and Monique said she would return my books for me if I get any off the bookmobile." No point mentioning that the Shady Grove library used death primarily as a way to increase its holdings. A pile of espionage novels arrived after the man in 124 departed, Betty noticed. She could make do with rereading her own favorite biographies until the bookmobile arrived next month.

"I plan to use what's here. I'm paying enough, after all," Betty couldn't help but add, and there was method to her cancellation of rides. If Sharon weren't spending time carting her around on errands, she would have more time for visits or for real outings.

Finally, during week three, Sharon arranged to come over for a whole afternoon. Betty put out her silver and Spode china and ordered scones from the food service. She ironed an embroidered tablecloth and napkins, talking aloud to Charlie as she eased the iron into the corners: "Look how I'm putting out our nicest things for our Sharon. She's coming over today for tea."

She positioned his photo toward the table. "There, now you won't miss a thing."

She was wearing a new fleece top printed with chickadees. The Velcro fastenings weren't to her liking and the fleece was stiff, but the aide who brought the catalog looked so hard worn that Betty had placed an order. It seemed like the least she could do.

Sharon arrived only a little late with a pot of pansies and Monique.

"Here's your visitor, Betty! Oh, look what your daughter brought you. You'll want to put these outdoors." Sharon was trying to set them on the table.

Monique went on, "Mother is adjusting. We've had a little talk about signing out." She added in a low voice, "I can give you details later."

Betty opened the hall door wide to give her a hint, which she took.

"Sounds like a college dorm, Mom." Sharon gave her a hug.

"Yes, with Monique as the housemother." Or warden, but there was no point in upsetting Sharon. Today was supposed to be fun.

Sharon brought her up to date on Vince's family; a first great-nephew had been born, and Betty was invited to the christening party. She described a new flan recipe she would do at her next pantry party. Betty agreed that it sounded novel. Then Betty got out old photo albums unearthed during her move. As they sat with the album on the pretty table, Betty felt like the stylish mother and daughter at tea in the brochure. In fact, she regretted hiding her guest away in her apartment instead of their being on display in the dayroom.

They pored over the photos.

"There's my graduation class." Betty pointed to herself in a smart suit and hat. "I was the valedictorian."

"Really? I didn't know that."

Sharon studied the photo and then Betty. Yes, the imprint of the young, oval face and large, pensive eyes was still there. Her mother had aged well, turning into the grandma of storybooks but without the grandchildren, unfortunately. At least her mother had never harped on that, in fact never even asked.

Betty continued her recollections, encouraged by the photograph. "The principal said I should go to training college to be a teacher."

"You didn't want to?"

"Pa said he didn't have money for sending girls to college." To get away from home, she got a job at Woolworth's as an assistant clerk in fabrics, she explained.

"You can't imagine the thrill of walking under the red sign with 'Woolworth's 5 and 10 Cents' on it in raised, gold letters. I earned enough money to buy pretty skirts and shirtwaists." Betty paused, thinking of one she had especially liked, red and white polka dotted.

"I wasn't much of a seamstress. The head clerk was a witch when I cut something wrong."

Sharon laughed as her mother described how she recommended ugly fabric on purpose to be moved to the candy counter.

"People bought a lot of loose candy in those days. I weighed out peanuts, malted milk balls, licorice, lemon drops, what have you. Then I'd put the candy in little white bags and ring it up on a big register. A girl was queen of her counter in those days."

"Then Dad came in, right, and gave you a hard time?"

"Yes, he told me he wanted one of each kind. That was a job of weighing and figuring. Of course, he thought I wouldn't be able to do it. Oh, he was so handsome in his army uniform."

They both glanced at his picture on the shelf. Charlie looked amused, eyebrow lifted slightly.

"By the time we got married, I had been promoted to working with the accountant in a little booth where you could look over the whole floor. Normally, it was a man's job."

Sweeping by the soda jerks and the other counter girls to climb to the accountant's office had been wonderful. "But finally when we knew you were coming, that was the end of working."

"But I remember you helped Dad sometimes with his paperwork. Wasn't I in junior high?" Sharon took her mother's hand.

"In fact, his company wanted to hire me." Sharon's nails were a dark plum today matching her sweater nicely. Betty stroked her fingers before saying, "It wouldn't have worked out though."

"Why not?" Sharon glanced at her dad's photo. It was kind of creepy the way the eyes seemed focused on them.

"Well, it just wouldn't have. And a girl needs a mother at home."

Betty saw no point in going into something so long gone by, how Charlie thought having her working would undermine one of his best sales pitches as a *family man*. That wasn't something a young woman—well, Sharon Lynne wasn't young anymore, she kept forgetting—wasn't something today's working woman would understand.

"I would have been fine. Besides, weren't you bored just cooking, grocery shopping, and cleaning?"

She had wished her mother would wear smart pedal-pushers like some of the other mothers and have a car during the day, not dress like Timmy's mother on *Lassie*, in a flowered apron and sweater. But since her father needed the car for business, it would have been hard for her mother to do much outside of home anyway, she supposed.

"You make it sound as if I was the hired girl." Betty dropped Sharon's hand.

"I didn't mean it that way. I just meant, didn't you want more for yourself? Why didn't you speak up?"

Betty shrugged. Her daughter had found her disappointing, as usual. Self-denial for family had been part of her satisfaction. She had always thought that part of one's *self* as a woman was making sure others were able to build their *selves*. Oh, it was hard to explain. Of course, there were many times she had wanted to smack Sharon for being demanding or to call Charlie a cheapskate, but *not* doing so had allowed her to build a little pile of chips to cash in from time to time at their expense. Not admirable, but a modest power play, like her move to Shady Grove, though it was beginning to look as if this investment wasn't going to pay off. Sharon had only been over once for a whole afternoon, and now she was getting touchy. Betty could tell she wouldn't be persuaded to stay longer today.

"This has been nice, Mom. Now, I've got to go to pick up something for Vince's dinner. Tonight's a demonstration at a bridal shower." Sharon gave her mother a quick hug.

"Thanks for coming over, honey." Then she couldn't resist saying as Sharon opened the door, "You should cook more for your own husband instead of strangers, dear."

"Fine, Mom. Yes, I should be a better homemaker." The sarcasm in her daughter's voice couldn't be missed.

After the door closed, Betty sat down to replay the conversation to figure out where it went wrong, where, once again, they had failed to make a perfect connection. Would Sharon have been happier to hear that, yes, she had wanted lots of things she never got—to go to college, to move somewhere else, or, or to go to England and see the royal palaces, or even just to work in one of the town offices, or well, she didn't know what all. There was a lot out there she had missed and wouldn't be finding now at Shady Grove, that's for sure. Would telling Sharon about her sacrifices have made her a more interesting mother, or Sharon a better wife, to put it bluntly?

On her way out, Sharon marched right by Monique. She didn't need to deal with that woman who treated her like the parent of a new kindergartener and, worse yet, her mother like a recalcitrant pupil. She sat in the car fuming. Yes, she should give more attention to Vince. Her lack there even showed to her mother apparently, and she already knew she was a bad daughter. Next time she visited, they would stay away from personal subjects and go to a movie instead.

For Betty, the evening stretched out. She turned down an invitation to learn to play canasta and tried to reread a biography of Jackie Kennedy. About nine, Vince called to let her know he would pick her up for her hair appointment on Monday.

"Oh, I'm not going to the NuLook anymore."

"Sharon said you've been canceling, but I'll take you. Won't be any trouble at all."

"You don't need to bother. They do hair right here."

"I bet you miss the girls at the NuLook. Come on, I'll take you. I should check on my work there anyway. Pick you up at the usual time."

Well, that would be something to look forward to from her old life. Vince was a brick.

7

An Unexpected Journey

*E*very Monday for years, Betty had gone to the NuLook Salon, where Michelle washed and styled her hair in the old-fashioned way. Betty favored upswept swoops at the sides that she could pin back to keep neat until the set started to give out. Though Michelle offered to restore her hair to its original auburn, Betty always refused.

Betty enjoyed listening to the younger stylists chat about who had said what, and what their boyfriends had or had not given them for their birthdays. Also, she kept up on all the troubles of Dolly, who owned the salon, and whose sons gave her no end of trouble, no matter that they were pretty much grown up. All had been arrested for one reason or another—the incidents were never their fault, of course. But Dolly supported each one when he needed it, often moving to the couch herself if her little house got too crowded with girlfriends or sisters of guys her sons knew and even their pets.

As she sat under the dryer, Betty leafed through glossy brochures. The better magazines were just out of reach, so she was stuck with some hair product advertisements and a couple of travel pamphlets. She flipped through one on rail travel. Each page showed a different city. Boston, Washington, Chicago, Seattle, Miami, San Francisco, all sparkled. Other photos showed the sleek engines and passenger cars touring through the best American landscapes. The seasons whirled in a kaleidoscopic color display—fall, winter, spring, and summer in America. Betty flipped along and stopped to read the page about accommodations. A silver-haired woman relaxed in a generous seat with her coffee on her tray table. A handsome conductor in a blue uniform was describing something in the lovely view out her window. The woman looked familiar in some way to Betty, a handsome woman, smart in a red sweater.

"Okay, Mrs. Miles, you're dry now," Michelle said as she pulled up the dryer hood and gave Betty a hand getting up. Betty settled at Michelle's station, absentmindedly carrying the magazines with her.

"How are you doing after your move?"

"I have things pretty well in order now," Betty said.

"I was afraid, after going to Shady Grove, you wouldn't be coming here," said Michelle, taking the last of the rollers out of Betty's hair. "How would you like this fixed today, Mrs. Miles? How about little curls?" She got out a curling iron.

"Oh, I'd look like I stuck a fork in my toaster. Just the usual." Betty was used to sleeping in a hair net to hold the waves in place. This worked at least until the weekend.

While Michelle tipped Betty's head down as she trimmed the back, Betty had a good look at the rail brochure. The woman in the travel photo looked so familiar, the pearl earrings and expensive-looking sweater, a confident and happy woman only a year or two younger than Betty. Could it be someone she knew? That didn't seem possible.

"Oh, are you taking a trip, Mrs. Miles?" Michelle leaned over Betty's shoulder for a better look at the magazine in her lap.

Suddenly, Betty knew where she had seen this woman before. She was in the brochure for Shady Grove, the lovely woman having tea with her daughter. And here she was enjoying more of the good life on a rail journey. "See America!" the caption read.

If this woman could go wherever she wanted, why shouldn't she go somewhere herself?

"Yes, I am!" Betty spoke quickly. "I won't be here next week, or the week after." She glanced at the brochure again. The vacation pass was good for several days of travel, with unlimited stops. "In fact, I'll just call you when I get back."

She was so anxious for Michelle to finish up, she almost caught her heel on the footrest when Michelle helped her down from the chair.

"You have a good time, Mrs. Miles. Send us a postcard," Dolly said as Betty left the salon. "And tell Vince my water heater needs adjusting again, I think."

Betty paid, tipped Michelle, and rushed out. Before she called Vince to come pick her up, she went to the travel agent down the strip mall to see about a ticket.

As it turned out, getting a reservation was easy.

"I'd like one of these See America tickets," she said when she got in the door. She held up the brochure. One of the agents took off her headset and invited Betty to sit down. Her phone rang every few minutes. She glanced back and forth between Betty, her computer, and the phone.

"Where would you like to go?"

Betty glanced at the brochure. The woman in the photo seemed to be going along a coastline.

"How about here?" She held up the brochure. "This looks lovely."

The agent took the brochure from her, saying the train could be the California Zephyr—Denver, Salt Lake City, Reno, and Emeryville—with a connection to the Coast Starlight. "Are you sure you shouldn't fly out there, ma'am?"

"I'm sure the train will be fine. Those places all sound lovely. Now, go ahead and set it up." She removed her credit card from the secret pocket in her purse and snapped it on the desk. The agent began typing obediently. Being decisive was so empowering!

"When would you like to travel, ma'am?"

"Soon. I'd like to leave, let's see, tomorrow."

"That soon? Let me see if anything's available. Do you want to make stops or go straight to California?"

"Well—" She had some cousins in the West somewhere. Were they still alive?

The agent turned more proactive. "Here's what I suggest. Buy the ticket for straight through. Then when you get to Chicago, where you have a long layover, you can think about making changes with agents there."

"What an excellent idea!" Betty put away her credit card, heart pounding, either from the excitement of travel or a heart attack. Best to wait and see.

The ticket popped out of a printer. "Here's your ticket. I booked you for a coach seat, but you may want to change that for a sleeper, if someone cancels." She handed an itinerary and the tickets to Betty who dropped first one and then the other. The agent came around the desk to retrieve them. "Are you sure you're up to this tomorrow, madam?"

"Of course I am." Whether this was true or not, time would tell, Betty thought. She called Vince from the travel agency and walked back to the NuLook where he would expect to find her. She waited outside to discourage Dolly from waylaying Vince about her water heater. No good would come of that in Betty's opinion.

Soon he drove up in the panel van. When he helped Betty into the front seat, she shoved aside coffee cups, a fry wrapper, and a couple of sandwich bags. It was obvious Sharon hadn't ridden in the panel van since the move.

"You're smiling. It must be a good hair day!" Vince said.

She felt like sharing the thrill of her ticket with him. Vince was a good sport, but of course he would tell Sharon. Then they would both come over. Then there would be a long discussion where everyone danced around what they really wanted to say. No, she would play it safe and just leave a note for them tomorrow.

"How was the hen party? Did they give advice about getting rid of no-good son-in-laws?"

"Oh, now! Get along with you," Betty said.

They pulled into the one-way drive at Shady Grove. As Vince helped her out he said, "We'll be putting in your closet shelving first thing tomorrow morning. Sharon's off until noon."

"Oh, there's no rush. I'll get settled here later sometime, I suppose."

He looked puzzled.

"You like it okay?"

"Oh, a person can get used to anything."

Vince didn't look convinced.

8

After Hours

*B*ack in his car alone, Vince turned over in his mind a recent evening he had spent at the NuLook for his sideline employment, remodeling work. The fact was that he had been there until past ten o'clock. Since Dolly was a sister of his brother's ex-wife, she and Vince were acquainted. Over the past month, he had put up new drywall after a minor blaze caused by the spontaneous combustion of chemical-covered cloths. This had evolved into updating the look of the front of the salon too. With more men coming in, Dolly decided to reduce the amount of pink for more silver and black. The other night, he had gone over to put on a second coat of paint, a job that should have taken about forty-five minutes.

Dolly often stayed while he worked. She checked the inventory in the back room, organized the magazines up front, and, last time, sat in one of the stylist's chairs and chatted while he painted. She wasn't young, just a few years shy of Sharon's 51, but unlike Sharon, for work Dolly wore short dresses and clicked around on high heels. He noticed her colored toenails always peeked out, even in winter. These days, she had red hair and was wearing it caught up in a big clip so that wisps fell around her face. This accentuated her large eyes, which often had dark circles. There were crow's-feet at the corners that her makeup didn't quite disguise, but she was a pretty woman, if one who looked like she had been worn hard.

"Aren't you here kind of late?" Vince said.

"Too much to think about at the house. Kids," Dolly said. "They drive me nuts. You're lucky you didn't have any."

"Maybe yes, maybe no."

"You know Teddy, my youngest, they gave him community service."

"Maybe he'll be okay now." Though he doubted it. Dolly had a knack for overlooking the obvious with her sons. You couldn't let them drop out of school and then expect miracles.

"I tell him to get a better job. Working in a pawn shop, what kind of place is that for a young man?"

"Maybe not the best." Vince put down the brush to rest his arm. He had always liked Teddy and remembered him as a little kid. Dolly and her kids had been at holiday dinners back before the divorce.

"Could you help him out, Vince? He and his dad just fight with each other when I send him over to work there."

"I've got a drywalling job coming up. Do you think he'd want in on that?"

"I'll make sure." Dolly smiled at him, nodding her head. "You should of had kids, Vince."

He finished up the last corner and pounded the covers back on the cans.

"Come on, sit down. I'll make you some hot chocolate."

Vince sat down gingerly in one of the stylist chairs that she pointed to. After she poured hot water over a package of chocolate, she pulled up a chair with a tray on it.

"I know, Vince, I'll give you a manicure." And before he could jump up, she pinned him in with her tray and reached for his hand. "It's the least I can do, if you'll take on Teddy," she said, shaking her red curls.

"Isn't this just for women?" Vince felt silly with his fingers in a dish of lotion.

"Manicures for men are getting more common. That's what my magazines say, though we don't do many yet."

"Maybe just for those gay guys," Vince said.

"Vince, aren't you stereotyping though!" Dolly said, working with the cuticle shaper. "Many men take care of themselves."

"But not in Elkhart." He winced as she worked at his right thumb.

"Well, maybe not here," she agreed, bending close over his hands, then taking them momentarily in hers.

While she worked, she chattered on about her favorite TV shows, things she had read in magazines about vitamins, and health advice for seniors to pass along to Betty.

He didn't really listen to it all but relaxed into the sound of her voice and the touch of her hands, a caring touch, someone paying close attention to a part of him.

"I've been reading this book called *Looking Younger*, you know?" She got out a trimmer and focused on his left hand. "Exercise. It says lots of smart people don't exercise."

"Probably too busy."

"I'm going to start exercising every day starting tomorrow. I'm on my feet all day here, but that's not exercise." She stretched her arms over her head and twisted to work out the stiffness. Smiling, she took his hand again. "This book, it also explains how women's bodies are different from men's. How women's brains react differently." She finished trimming and got out a buffing tool.

This is something Vince has known for a fact since he got married. Women could pack away details about the most tiresome stuff and expect you to take an interest too. Sharon just assumes, for instance, that he should know which clothes go together in the washer. Of course, she has explained to him about a million times and even put a sign on the washing machine. But he can't be bothered with actually carrying out the instructions. Just throw the stuff in and turn it on. Case closed.

"There, that's about all I can do." As she held her hands under his to show off the trimmed nails, her thumbs grazed his palms. "You could take better care of yourself, Vince." Dolly smiled up at him under her curled lashes.

He got out of the chair and put his tools together hurriedly before, well, he wasn't sure what, but it sounded attractive.

"I'll check that water heater thermostat one more time. Maybe, uh, Wednesday night," he called as he left.

9
Charlie's Surprise

*I*n her freshly styled hair, Betty tried to make a quick reentry to Shady Grove, but Monique waved the clipboard for her to sign in. Obediently Betty filled in the time of return while being reminded that a hair salon was available on-site. As if the ticket in her purse would set off a security sensor, Betty was anxious to get back to her apartment.

Safely inside her quarters, she laid the ticket on the table, admiring the red and blue insignia—her ticket to ride. She hummed the Beatles tune while putting away her purse.

Though telling Sharon was out of the question, Charlie could be let in on her surprise. But facing the photo, she found she couldn't seem to say out loud in her living room the little speech in her head that outlined the logical chain of events leading to this ticket.

Instead, she began tentatively, "I think I deserve a little vacation, don't you?"

He said nothing.

"I'm considering going away on a trip—but for just a day or so, probably."

Joyce Hicks

Her heart rolled over with an uneven thump as she delivered her news with its little white lie. There, she had told him. He seemed surprised, an eyebrow raised.

Then as she was gauging his reaction, someone knocked at the door and opened it gently.

"Here's your mail. You forgot to pick it up." Her favorite aide held out a bundle. Betty thanked her, tamping down the urge to show her the ticket.

The spell of her interchange with Charlie broken, Betty sorted the mail pile eagerly. Even a new sweepstakes entry would be welcome. *But what's this?* A cream-colored envelope stamped CONFIDENTIAL for Mr. Charles Miles at the address of his last employer. The address of the duplex had been scribbled on it, and the post office had forwarded the envelope to Shady Grove.

What in the world! She examined the return address and postmark: First Capital Bank, Personal Banking, from Chicago, mailed a week before.

"Of all the darn things! This is mailed to you, you turkey," she addressed the photo in mild irritation, "and you're not here to deal with it."

Their bank, Social Security, and his pension organization to notify, death certificate copies to distribute, subscriptions to cancel, and endless bills to pay for her rite of passage to widowhood had angered her more than once. Why did he have to go and die, causing hateful red tape to attend to? she had often griped. She ripped open the envelope and scanned the page.

> *Referring to the safe deposit box #6792, the 25-year term of rental has expired. Payment has been in arrears for 12 months. After non-contact of 5 years*

84

> *by you or legal heirs, the contents will be remitted to*
> *the State of Illinois.*

Betty read it again, word by word, like a third grader. A safe deposit box in Chicago, at a bank she had never heard of. She set the letter down in front of her husband's photo.

"What is this, Charlie?" She addressed the cocked eyebrow, the lips ready to smile. *But had there always been a slight rise in his lip on the left side*? Almost disdainful.

Betty picked up the photo and held it a few inches from her face, focusing on the upturn of the lip until the curve dissolved into grey lines and fuzz, but no answer presented itself for the change in expression. It was just a crazy idea. But so was an unknown safe deposit box at a Chicago bank! Why, they had done all their banking right here at home at First Farm Trust, well, before it changed its name, twice, to . . . First Something-or-Other.

Betty got to the phone to call Sharon. About to press speed dial, she set the phone back on its base.

No, not yet.

She strode in the tight perimeter of her apartment, upbraiding herself for opening the letter at all. Her whole life had been patterned after the sage advice "Never borrow trouble." Optimism, compliance, selflessness, acceptance were all virtues she lived by that stemmed from this adage. Now here was trouble arriving in an envelope not addressed to her, not meant for her at all. At the least, it was business papers to attend to, something or other that had to be conveyed to somebody or other.

At the worst. Well, who knew . . . an IOU for an unpaid debt? He had been a man who liked a wager. Would some awful people come after her? Someone named Knuckles, or Baby Face?

Just then, she saw a black car stop along the driveway opposite her patio. A man got out, leaning on the car to make a phone call. She stared at her own phone, but it remained silent. The man got back in, and the car pulled away.

Perhaps the odds and ends from Charlie's desk would reveal something. Betty turned to head to the desk in the corner, but of course the corner was in her duplex and the desk now in storage.

She circled her kitchen-living room again and again and returned to the table where her eye fell on the rail ticket. It seemed impossible that only ten minutes ago she had feared announcing her surprise trip to her empty living room.

The time for pussyfooting around was over. She picked up the ticket and shook it in front of her husband's photo.

"Did I mention I'm going to Chicago? Chicago, Illinois?"

Absolutely, the photo changed. The slight twinkle and the raised eyebrow, formerly portents to a laugh, now expressed alarm, pure and simple.

"Don't you wish you were here now?" She stared at the upturned lip again.

"I can see I'll have to look into that lockbox myself." She yanked open a kitchen cabinet drawer and put him under the placemats, giving the drawer a hard shove closed with her hip. She needed to pack.

First, she got out her navy pocketbook with the three compartments and the triple gold clasps on the top, even though Sharon said only Queen Elizabeth carried a bag like that anymore. Obviously, she and her namesake knew a good handbag when they saw one! The fat center section was good for a wallet, her ticket, pencil, tiny notebook, and a hankie, though nowadays she used tissues, of course. Into one side pocket she counted out extra medication because you should never assume your luggage would get there. In the other side pocket went the letter and a copy of Charlie's death certificate. Who knew if she would have to produce this final chapter, again.

Lastly, what to do about letting Sharon know about her travels? A note would do, a note to find when she and Vince came tomorrow to install the closet shelving. Calling, of course, would be more polite, but an argument would ensue about the dangers, her health, or her lack of travel experience.

They would provide endless suggestions like "Just telephone the bank, for heaven's sake," and if she wanted to travel, "Why not go to Branson, Missouri, with the Shady Grove group?"

Overdressed women throwing panties at a shoe-polish haired has-been at ten in the morning? *NO THANK YOU!*

"Sometime you can fly to see your cousin out West."

No, Betty didn't care for flying. With the train, you could see things along the way. Besides, with plenty of time for conversation, sometimes you met interesting companions. She remembered the lovely trips she and Charlie had taken right after the War.

For certain, by the time the conversation ended, she would be going nowhere because she wouldn't want to worry Sharon. So she began to pack a single suitcase. What wouldn't fit in it, she would buy.

She laid out several suits and put them back in the closet. Instead, she chose her blue suit with its elastic-waist skirt to wear on the train, a white polyester blouse, and the jacket. She would pack the slacks for another day. Her pajamas, pills, toothbrush, botanicals shirt, and shirt with cardinals filled the small case.

Well, time to write the letter, but she realized she had no notepaper. She shuffled through the trash, finding envelopes she could tear open to make some paper. Never much of a writer, Betty decided she just needed to be loving and firm. In fact, Sharon and Vince might be glad to have her out of the way for a few weeks, though they wouldn't say so.

> Dear Sharon,
>
> I love you very much, but I have decided to take a journey. Don't worry about me. Thanks for everything.
>
> Love, Mother

Goodness, this sounded like a suicide note! Betty wadded up the paper.

> Dear Sharon and Vince,
>
> By the time you read this, I will be far away. Don't try to contact me, I'll call you when I get there.
>
> Love, Mother

This one sounded as if she had killed somebody or embezzled and was on the lam. She crumpled it in disgust.

Perhaps being direct was best.

> Dear Sharon,
>
> I need a little change of scene. I have decided to take a train trip across country. Thanks for all the help you have given me lately. Don't worry about me. I will call you soon.
>
> Love, Mother

There, this one sounded better, direct, and appreciative. She propped up the acceptable note on her dresser and tossed the rejects in the recycle bin, then took it down the hall to the refuse area herself. There was no point in leaving trash around until an aide emptied it.

One problem remained: how to get out without signing out. Just waltzing quickly by the front desk was impossible. She simply wasn't fast enough. Beyond the lawn next to her patio door was a driveway—that she could reach without being waylaid.

Simple. She pressed speed dial on her phone.

"Hello, Mabel? Can you be here in the back drive at seven tomorrow morning?"

"No, not for breakfast. I'm making a getaway." A little intrigue would ensure Mabel's cooperation as an accessory. They agreed on the details.

After supper in the dining room where Betty barely hid her excitement—in fact, Paul said she *glowed*—she set her alarm for five thirty in the morning, took a bath in the shower/bath tank, and went to bed.

10
The Escape

By six the next morning, Betty had made toast and coffee and packed two peanut butter sandwiches and a banana. She sat at her table looking around at the apartment. She almost tore up her note and called Mabel to cancel. What was she thinking, running off this way! Didn't she owe Sharon more than this?

But what about Mary Grace's neighbor waiting for the funeral home director to show up? If she were destined to land at the bottom of her shower/bath tank, out of reach of the buzzer (with no poodle for company), at least she wanted to live a little first.

Mabel arrived early at six thirty, the engine on her Pontiac growling as she pumped the accelerator, while Betty bumped her red suitcase along the patio. It followed her obediently on its little wheels over the lawn and to the car.

"Hurry up and get in!"

"For pity's sakes, quit racing the engine."

When Mabel jerked the car into gear, Betty got her foot in just before the heavy door slammed. Without a seatbelt on yet, she flopped over the bench seat onto to her friend, sending them both into giggles. Then she reached over Mabel's arm. "I'm going to blow the horn!"

"You go girl!" screamed Mabel. The Pontiac barreled out the one-way drive past the *No Outlet* sign into the free world.

Though Betty had not been inside the train station in years, she recalled that it had a waiting room and ticket agent, but today, from the outside, it looked deserted. Maybe everything she's heard lately about the demise of rail was true.

Before she could flag down Mabel with a change of heart, the Pontiac pulled way in a spray of gravel. With only her rolling suitcase for a pal, Betty shoved open the door.

"Well, no shit," a woman said loudly. Betty hesitated. Cell phone gripped under her chin, the woman held the door and bumped Betty's suitcase over the threshold.

"Let me get that for you, hon," she addressed Betty then her caller. "You just tell them I don't want to hear any more crap. I'm not working nights next week. Love ya. Bye."

Then she settled Betty into one of the blue plastic chairs, her cell phone snapping shut. Betty would have chosen a different seat, but she felt she shouldn't move now.

"Call me Lou. You might want to take off that coat. This train is always late. Service is crappy, you know."

"Is it?" Betty asked. Though this wasn't the sort of woman she usually was on a first-name basis with, she introduced herself.

Betty appraised her companion by turning, pretending to look for the clock, and was startled to discover Lou was only a few years younger than herself. Her black hair was cut like a boy's and stood up straight. She wore jeans, knee-high boots, and a suede jacket.

A few other passengers sat in the plastic chairs lining the perimeter of the room. A few red chairs sat in the middle. Betty's chair faced the station agent's window that was closed, and the coffee shop that she had seen in the Eisenhower administration had been replaced by a vending machine.

Uncertain whether to check in, she got up and knocked on the plywood over the agent's window.

"There's no agent here anymore." Other passengers took interest in their new companion, obviously an ingénue.

"I do have a reservation, but what about my suitcase?"

"The conductor will take it on the train for you. Unless it weighs more than fifty pounds."

"Oh, no, it doesn't." Betty looked out the window down the tracks. "We just wait in here? When does the train come?"

"When it feels like it!" A general guffawing spread among the travelers.

Betty felt a lump rising in her throat. Maybe Sharon would be right. She just wasn't up to this sort of adventure.

"Don't worry, ma'am. I'm tracking the train with my phone. It was spotted in Waterloo already by my niece. Another half an hour, it'll be here."

Betty began to survey her companions to see just what she was getting into. Lou was making more phone calls peppered with words Betty didn't ordinarily use. Across the way was a man buried in his coat. He snored loudly. Then there were a couple of young people, college students she judged.

Both wore those music gadgets with the earplugs. Betty smiled remembering an aunt who was hard of hearing but much too proud for hearing aides. "Why don't you people speak up?" she would shout across the Thanksgiving table. Two other women waiting discussed their grandchildren.

Lou turned to Betty looking her over, "That's not a bad getup for the train."

"It seemed like I should choose something that doesn't wrinkle." Betty smoothed down her navy skirt.

"That little blue hat really makes the outfit. You'll get a good seat. They'll think you're a nun." Lou leaned over to check out Betty's crepe-soled, tie shoes.

"Certainly, not. I'm a Methodist." Betty took off her hat and looked at it.

After getting to know the crowd, she noticed the time. It was nine o'clock, time for Sharon and Vince to arrive at Shady Grove.

11

On the Lam

Sharon gave a tap on the door. No answer. So she knocked again. Perhaps her mother was in the bathroom. She stood waiting in the corridor and knocked again, but Betty did not appear. Finally, she got out her duplicate key, though she suspected this kind of entry was against the rules.

"Mother, we're here."

Silence filled the dim room. Sharon opened the drapes so she could see better, then started toward the bedroom but held back. Lifelessness came from it like a cold breeze. She told herself to get a grip, but she couldn't bring herself to go into the bedroom. How many times had she listened sympathetically to clients tell disaster stories in which parents fell in bathtubs, tripped over throw rugs, electrocuted themselves, mixed up their medication, rewrote their wills, or even married gold diggers or bigamists.

Sharon went back outside to the van, after checking the dining room and various other public rooms.

"Vince, come inside. I can't find her." They reentered the apartment together. Vince strode into the bedroom to find it empty, as was the bathroom, leaving at least the first level of Sharon's fears unfounded.

"Maybe she's visiting another apartment," said Vince. They sat down to wait, until Sharon finally went to check with the two other residents her mother had mentioned. No one had seen her since last night.

"Maybe she's taking a walk." Vince looked out the patio door across the lawn to the driveway.

"Now, where do you think she could she walk from here?" Sharon said. "Along the main road?"

"I'll check the property here and drive around the parking lot."

Soon Vince returned without a passenger to learn that Sharon had alerted Monique.

"She said they have a protocol for a resident search. It will take about twenty minutes." Sharon paced around picking up her mother's things and putting them down, remarking that her dad's photo wasn't on the bookcase.

Meanwhile back at the station, the excitement built as confirmation came via someone's cell phone that the train was approaching, and a boy reported seeing the light down the tracks.

Betty gathered her things. Hoisting her navy purse on her shoulder, she grabbed the handbag with her lunch she planned to keep with her on the train. Lou rolled her suitcase out the door with a reminder: "When you get to the conductor, remember to look fragile, so you get a good seat." They walked out to the tracks.

"Maybe we can sit together?" The enormity of what she was doing was beginning to dawn on Betty, and the woman was a distraction from the flutter of panic. But Lou was lingering behind for a last cigarette and talking to the young people.

"Dropped like a hot potato." Betty held her purse tight to her chest.

—⚋—

Back at the apartment, action was speeding up. Monique arrived to say that all areas had been searched, and no one found Betty.

"I thought you people were supposed to keep track of the residents at all times!" Sharon knew this was unreasonable and nasty, but it felt good to be a difficult person.

"Your mother was in assisted living, not memory care that is secured."

"*Was?*"

"As I wanted to discuss with you last week, she has not cooperated about signing out. Now, I'm sure there's a clue here to her whereabouts. Our policy is not to alert law enforcement until we feel satisfied we have checked all the premises. Let me just check through her things."

"Thank you, no. For now, I'll do it."

Vince gently urged Monique to let Sharon look on her own, promising to come to her office when they found something significant.

Sharon discovered her mother's favorite purse was gone, and crumbs were around the toaster.

"Mother would never leave the counter dirty overnight. She must have made toast this morning."

"There's got to be a reasonable explanation, honey," Vince said, thinking of how the day was disappearing. He had planned to clean his gutters. "I'll just bring in the shelving while we wait. Maybe she slipped by the desk people and went out for breakfast with a friend."

"Now, who would that be?" Sharon marched a tight circle around Vince. "You don't suppose she's out with that awful Mabel, do you?" Sharon didn't see how in good conscience her family let the woman drive, but possibly she had no family to monitor her.

"Maybe mother put her number in her address book." Sharon found the little red book and flipped though it page by page since she had no idea of Mabel's last name.

After carrying in the shelves, Vince went to the dresser to set aside the package of screws. There he found the note in Betty's schoolgirl hand and wordlessly handed it to Sharon.

She read it aloud.

> *Dear Sharon,*
>
> *I love you very much, but I have decided to take a journey. Don't worry about me. Thanks for everything.*
>
> *Love, Mother*

They looked in silence at the flattened envelope and the careful handwriting.

"Well, that explains it," said Vince. This was just another example of how women outfox you.

Sharon studied the note, turning the torn envelope in her hands, thinking of her mother's habits that ordinarily ran like clockwork. Where would she go? *On a journey?*

"Mother doesn't like to travel. Remember how she was about the cruise we tried to give her?"

"I don't think she wanted to go on water."

"Mother never does anything without checking with me first." Sharon spoke in a rising pitch. "We have all these perfect arrangements made for her *here*."

"She could have had something else in mind." He was beginning to recall the conversation they'd had when he picked her up at the beauty parlor.

"Vince!" Sharon began to pull on the cuff of her jacket sleeve. "You don't think it's possible she's committed suicide?" Sharon whirled around looking under the bed and even in the dresser drawers. "Oh, I knew she didn't really want to move to Shady Grove." She sat down on the bed, her fingers pressing her forehead.

"Killed herself?"

Although he hadn't said so, Vince had thought of this solution should anyone suggest that he move to Shady Grove. "No, honey, I don't think so. What did she say in the note? Read it again."

"She said she is taking a journey and that she loves me and not to worry. *Journey* could be a euphemism."

"You mean like a vacation to that place in Mexico?"

"No, like dying, Vince! The hospice people sometimes say something like that. 'We're here to help on the journey.'" Sharon began to roll up the edge of her jacket as she sat on the edge of the bed. "Look in the front closet, Vince. She's . . . she's not in there, is she?"

He stood back from the door and opened it carefully. He recalled his mother-in-law's comments when he had dropped her off from the beauty parlor. The closet was empty.

"How would Mother go about doing such a thing? Pills. Maybe she stashed the painkillers from her sprained ankle." Would her mother just take a pile of pills? Perhaps she had wandered off somewhere after taking pills and right now was lying unconscious behind a hedge. They should go out to look again, but where?

"Let's call the police," Sharon said.

Down the track Betty and Lou could see the Lakeshore Limited bearing down on them, horn wailing as it neared the grade crossing—two longs, one short, one long. The enormous engine, its blue and grey nose with a round light like a giant eye, gave Betty a thrill she hadn't felt in years: fear, excitement, patriotic fervor. It was nearly a sexual experience. Heart soaring now, she pushed ahead of the other travelers.

Blue uniformed personnel got off, some of them women to Betty's surprise, and hollered instructions to the passengers. A conductor took her arm and bags to help her up the steps. Betty watched despairingly as Lou swung her way into a different car.

"Right this way, ma'am. Let's find you a good seat." They wormed their way along the blue carpet, past passengers standing up for a stretch who leaned into seats to let the pair by. After an empty car, they passed into another car that was a sea of blue and black. The conductor led her toward an empty seat on the aisle.

Finally, he said, "How about here, Sister?" He handed Betty into the seat and placed her carry-on bag at her feet and suitcase above on the rack.

Betty turned to say "How do you do" to her seatmate. She also was dressed in dark blue and black, an Amish woman about Betty's own age, who smiled and arranged her long blue skirt to make room for Betty's shorter one. Yes, maybe her sensible navy suit would have to go.

Pretending to be looking out the windows and for the restroom, Betty surveyed these traveling companions. In the other seats were an Amish mother and father, two girls in their black bonnets, two boys holding straw hats, and a young couple with a baby, also in a black bonnet. Well, these were as interesting traveling companions as anyone could ask for. Betty settled in to enjoy herself.

When Sharon had her hand on the phone to call the police, Vince said, "Wait a minute. Let's just look around again. Maybe there's some clue we missed here."

Sharon rechecked the closet and realized her mother's favorite suit was missing. Would she make toast and put on her navy suit and blue hat before swallowing pills? But her mother believed in dressing properly for any occasion. She would never want to be found in a state of dishabille.

"Please call 9-1-1, Vince. We've waited long enough. This is so, so annoying."

Sharon could see the headline now: "Woman Disappears" followed by "Elizabeth Miles, mother of Sharon D'Angelo, family care specialist at County Hospital, has disappeared and is presumed dead in her blue suit." Sharon's panic had given way to irritation and was headed for guilt. How could she, a daughter, have let this happen?

Vince explained the situation to the dispatcher and within minutes two squad cars pulled up, blocking off the driveway behind the patios. Sharon gave a description of her mother to two officers, when she had last been seen, her medical conditions, and so forth. They checked for signs of forced entry through the patio door. The police were polite, but Sharon could tell that they felt she should not have lost her mother.

They looked around the apartment. "Did you move anything or empty that kitchen recycling bin this morning, ma'am?" They noticed it was empty.

"No, but my Mother might have." This was good news. Would a woman bent on killing herself carry down the recycling?

"Let's just have a look in the trash. Is it down the hall?"

Monique had reappeared and led the way to the recycling closet, murmuring that residents weren't supposed to dispose of their own recycling.

Betty's bag was right on top. The officers pulled out everything, an old TV guide, advertisements, and solicitation letters. They leafed through a direct-mail contest that Betty had filled out. Vince concurred with his mother-in-law on the sports car chosen for her runner-up prize, though Sharon was appalled that her mother had devoted so much time to this come-on and then thrown it out. Within a few minutes, another of Betty's notes turned up. An officer read aloud as if to an assembly:

Dear Sharon and Vince,

> *By the time you read this, I will be far away. Don't try to contact me, I'll call you when I get there.*
>
> *Love, Mother*

He turned to Sharon, "Does she have any reason to run off and not tell you where?"

"Of course not." Sharon didn't like the implication in his tone. Her mother was not a felon. Monique too looked at Sharon. She glared back.

They leafed through the last of the bag, finding the final note stuck with orange peels.

This time the officer read silently and turned it over to Sharon. "Looks like the mystery is solved, ma'am."

She snatched it from him and read to Vince and Monique:

Dear Sharon,

> *I need a little change of scene. I have decided to take a train trip across country. Thanks for all the help you have given me lately. Don't worry about me. I will call you soon.*
>
> *Love, Mother*

"Of course, she meant to leave me this note!"

Sharon recovered her manners, while hustling the police toward the patio door. "Thank you so much for your help."

"So, Mom's on the lam!" said one officer. "Call us if you don't hear from her within twenty-four hours."

"Looks to me like someone wasn't too happy here at Shady Grove," the other officer observed within earshot of Monique, who was already in a state over all the paperwork this incident would cause.

The two men stopped outside the door. "Look there, Ms. D'Angelo. I'd say your mom rolled a suitcase right over the grass early this morning." Faint wheel lines still showed. "Probably a friend or cab picked her up. You could call and see."

Sharon examined the grass, and then closed the patio door on the police and the hallway door on Monique.

"Well, that's that," said Vince, flopping into the electric chair and reaching for the television remote.

"What do you mean? We can't let Mother take a trip on the train. She's not strong enough for that. Suppose she gets confused. Suppose she falls?" Sharon pictured a new head-line: 'Mother Escapes into the Sunset on a Rail Journey.' "Besides, she's supposed to be settling in here at Shady Grove."

"I thought maybe she was having second thoughts about that," Vince said as he used the power control to recline the chair.

"Why do you say that?"

"When I picked her up at the beauty parlor she said something about getting set up later.

"You didn't tell me that."

"I didn't think about it."

"Vince, I've been working on this for a year, trying to get her to make this decision. This morning I thought she was dead. *Now* you tell me, she's been telling you she doesn't like it here."

"Well, she didn't say that. She just didn't sound excited about it."

"What exactly did she say? Tell me exactly." Sharon yanked the power control and tilted him upright.

"I don't remember exactly. Don't give me the third degree." Even-tempered Vince had his limits. "If you wanted to know exactly how she felt about it, you should have asked her."

Sharon paced around. The man was maddening sometimes. He could pay the closest attention to the detail of the finest carpentry but only provide an overview of other kinds of things. Besides, what did he know about asking people about their feelings? Had he ever listened when she tried to tell him her feelings?

"I'm going to call that Mabel woman."

Her evasive answers confirmed her part in Betty's escapade—Sharon would not think of it in any other term, such as *escape*.

"Can you believe that woman said it was none of my business where Mother was going! 'Somewhere away,' she put it."

"All west-bound passenger trains that go through here in the morning stop in Chicago," offered Vince. "I think the east-bound come here at night."

Sharon got on the phone with Amtrak. Pretending to be her mother and providing a credit card number, she found that Betty had indeed bought a See America pass, with the first stop in Chicago.

"I want us to go to Chicago."

"Now?"

"Maybe if we leave now, we can catch Mother before she gets on any other train."

Vince offered various arguments—the distance involved, the unlikelihood of finding Betty, the gutters he was planning on cleaning—but he knew it was useless. They returned to their house and got Sharon's sedan. She filled an over-night bag with their toothbrushes, pajamas, and a change of clothes in spite of further protests from Vince. He saw it was definitely one of those *shut-up-and-drive* situations.

—m—

Meanwhile, Betty was settling into her first rail journey in over fifty years. She tucked her handbag at her feet and wiggled out of her coat. Her hat she tucked into the pocket of the seatback facing her. Perhaps she would just leave it there. She noted the button for lowering her seat back, but she didn't try it out yet. At the end of the car a lighted sign said Restroom, but with the way the car rocked back and forth, she wondered whether she could make it down there without an upset. She noted that the Amish lady had an old-fashioned wooden traveling box at her feet. Betty decided to see if she spoke English. Many who lived around Elkhart did not.

"Where are you going?"

"We're going on vacation, ya, on vacation to Glacier National Park." The woman adjusted her rimless glasses and smiled.

This settled it for Betty; if the Amish could go on vacation, certainly she could. If they could leave their buggies and navigate America, certainly she, who used to drive a car and today could program her VCR, could take a train trip.

"Where are you going?"

Though Betty didn't believe in giving strangers details, it seemed all right to chat with this lady. "I'm taking a trip West, but I'm not sure where I'm going yet." Betty was surprised to find she couldn't go on. Tears had formed in her eyes. She used her tissue to try to keep them in place. "I'm escaping from my daughter, I guess you could say." She tried to laugh.

"Uh-oh. Your daughter?" The woman looked around the train, perhaps thinking she was there somewhere.

"Yes, she wanted me to move to an assisted living place, which I did, but it's so boring. I don't suppose your old people move into those."

"No, just the English."

"Do you live on your own farm?" Betty had seen plenty of Amish farms in Indiana, neat white houses, black buggies lined up in the barns, more of a throwback to the nineteenth century than her own father's farm.

"No, I gave it to my sons when my husband died. Now I live with a daughter."

Betty pondered the Amish solution to old age. "So, you aren't alone then."

"There are nine of us in the house. My daughter works at a restaurant and her husband in the custom cabinet works. I do the housework and the cooking, washing, and mind the little ones." Betty had had enough of this sort of work when she was a girl.

"And the quilting?" She was watching the two youngest children who were misbehaving in their miniature black and blue garb like any children cooped up on a train.

The woman laughed. "Who has time for that? We buy from the store."

Nature was calling and couldn't be ignored any longer, so Betty cautiously made her way toward the restroom, slowly moving from one seatback to the next. The odor of ammonia and cleaning fluid would have told even a blind woman that she was in the right place. Betty could barely slide open the heavy door, then pushed it closed, and turned the locking handle toward red, wondering if she would ever get out again. Next she evaluated the metal toilet with its damp black seat. Already living dangerously, she decided consternation over this was useless. She closed her eyes and sat down. Thankfully, the sink had soap and even hot water, though all the towels were gone. Teetering back and forth, she was able to rearrange her clothes properly and finally forced the metal handle toward open.

With Chicago only about an hour away, she decided to eat her lunch. As she opened her sack, her seatmate opened the large wooden box, which contained a picnic spread Betty hadn't seen since haying time in the 1930s. Betty got out her two slices of bread with peanut butter, thinking her lunch wasn't much of a comment on the English, but her seatmate waved away her paper sack, handing her a sandwich of home-cured sausage on thick bread with a slather of hot mustard. Next came the deviled eggs, celery, and carrots with pickle spears. Soon, the daughter in the next seat opened a large jar of chicken and noodles, doling out plasticware to everyone, Betty included. Next came coffee from someone else's box with metal cups handed round. When Betty thought she couldn't take another bite, bags of oatmeal cookies appeared.

"You must have gotten up early to get all this together."

"Oh, ya, every day. I get up at 4:15. Monday laundry, Tuesday baking, Wednesday mending, Thursday is ladies' aide day, Friday cleaning, Saturday shopping." This took Betty right back to her mother's schedule. She was not at all sure that the promise of an old age with family was an even trade for this sort of slaving.

Stuffed and snoozing, Betty decided the Plain People could have all that work if they wanted it. The Merry Widows at Shady Grove had the right idea.

12
Tell it to the Judge

Betty's train was ahead of Sharon and Vince, but the couple had made good time. Vince was resigned to the journey. They had not been talking much because Sharon was making out order forms for her business. The monotony of driving the Indiana tollway gave Vince free time to think around the edges of a problem he was having—deviousness that he had never engaged in before. The trips to the NuLook to check on carpentry and plumbing were frequent and often unnecessary. When Dolly mentioned she intended to hang a new mirror, he volunteered to do it. After completing a drywalled area, he returned to sand down and repaint a section that looked a tiny bit rough. His promise to recheck, again, the connections around her new water heater made him squirm. Conscientiousness was a trademark of his work, but he knew he was going overboard. He glanced at his hands on the steering wheel; Sharon hadn't noticed the manicure, so there was no explaining to do yet.

Being around Dolly was so easy. She seemed to take anything that came along—good luck, bad luck—with the same acceptance, without worrying it to death. She talked a lot like most women, but she didn't seem to talk at him, or give so many details that he was just about to die, or go over plans with him until he could hardly breathe. She seemed to just let things happen, though of course some of the things she let happen were just plain dumb, such as giving her credit card to her oldest son so he could get through the week. No wonder she now had a sky-high balance. If Sharon had ever seen a balance that high, she would have insisted on many sacrifices to pay it off quickly.

While he pondered silently, Sharon used her cell phone apps and, as they crossed the Skyway Bridge, announced that she had a game plan all worked out. There was a parking garage next to Union Station. They would park and then go inside to find her mother. Vince pointed out that, in a huge station, this was like looking for a needle in a haystack, but Sharon was sure passengers waiting for trains going out in the evening would have a waiting room somewhere. She even called Amtrak to confirm her assumption. Of course, there was a waiting area for long-distance passengers.

"I'm sure we'll find Mother huddled somewhere eating one of those horrible peanut butter sandwiches she always carries if she goes anywhere for even the morning."

"Maybe she'll find a restaurant." He hoped so.

"Oh, imagine her going out to look for a restaurant in a city." She pictured her mother with her big, navy purse hanging off her arm, standing uncertainly, peering out over her bifocals at the traffic. What a perfect target for a mugger!

"There's probably somewhere to eat right in the train station." Vince felt he owed Sharon some comfort since she was holding him responsible for not reporting her mother's flight plan. Not that he knew it exactly, but he felt a miasma of guilt anyway.

"It'll have to be one that carries cinnamon rolls! You know how I can't get her to order anything substantial at a restaurant. And here she'd have to pay for it herself."

"I'm sure we'll find her, honey. Maybe I can get them to page her." Vince felt being positive was called for here.

—⚏—

Betty woke from a catnap as the train glided into the station. On the one hand, she felt excited. On the other, this whole thing was terrifying. What business did she have going off on her own like this? Suppose she fell sick; no one would know who she was. Of course, she had been to Chicago years ago but only to a couple of hotels, department stores, and once a theater. Fortunately, a rail magazine in the seat pocket had provided her with a few modern landmarks. Since the western train didn't leave until early evening, she had plenty of time go to the bank. Perhaps she could even visit the Sears Tower first. Everyone had heard about this famous building, and the magazine said it was right near the station. Looking for it would mean going out into traffic, but with something so large, how could she miss it?

The train pulled in. The Amish passengers closed up their boxes and put on their capes. The children were corralled. Betty and the Amish let the other passengers get off first. Then she got her purse, carry-on bag, and rolling suitcase, and made her way down the car and off onto the platform where people pressed toward the doors leading into the station.

Through the doors were the biggest crowds Betty had seen in years, suburban commuters as well as travelers. She was swept one way and then the other in the low-ceilinged passageways. She was part of the school of humanity that moved like a single organism, growing and ebbing—North Concourse, South Concourse, Ground Transportation, Adams Street. She rode up, then down an escalator.

A lobby, that's what she needed. She seemed to be walking up a slight slope and a lighted room was ahead. A few more yards and she stepped into the Grand Hall of the station. Columns soared, accentuating the scale of the room; at last, a rail station the way it should be. With the light and airiness, Betty's heart opened too. Never mind if she had a heart attack alone in a big city, there must be hospitals here. She had a place to go too, like all these people. She had a train to catch.

Sharon got herself and Vince to the station. She found the enter sign for the parking garage. She found the elevator down to the Amtrak level of the station. She guided them through the Saturday crowd right to the Amtrak ticket windows. No, they could not look up a name without some form of identification related to that party. But if such a person had purchased such a rail pass, she would most likely be getting on the western-bound train that departed later that night, or possibly a southern train. The other shorter trips would not be good use of a See America pass. Sharon pondered the points of the compass. West seemed more likely, so her mother must be here somewhere waiting for the departure of the Pacific Limited. They simply had to wander around and look for her. If they didn't find her within a reasonable length of time, they would try to get her paged.

"Of course, Mother would not agree to a cell phone," Sharon said. "I could just call her. Or you!" She turned to her husband. "You should have a cell phone, not just that pager." Tension made Sharon seek fault anywhere it could be found. Vince nodded, thinking that sometimes it was better not to be available during the day. Anyway, he despised those little devices that were a permanent attachment on many women's ears, and men too for that matter.

"I don't think she could get used to one of those anyway," Sharon said. "Remember how much trouble she had with running the VCR?"

—⁓—

Betty sat on a bench for a while in the Grand Hall to get her bearings and simply watch the people. Those with families made her think of when Sharon had been little. One time, they had gone on a driving trip to Florida, before Disney World, of course, packing their station wagon with a tent, Sterno stove, and so forth, to stop nights at camp parks, but the place Sharon had liked the best was a motel with cabins that looked like tepees. They scrimped on other parts of the trip so they could afford to stay. Inside were beds downstairs for the parents and, up above in the pointed part, a loft for children to sleep. Sharon had been afraid to go up the ladder until Betty said she would sleep up there too. She had hardly fit, but finally they dropped off to sleep back-to-back.

She was deeply sorry Sharon had not been able to enjoy these same pleasures as a parent, but some things were not to be. Warmth flooded her heart for her Sharon Lynne, and she tamped down the guilt over the hasty departure by deciding she would give Sharon a call tonight just before the train left. Maybe this time she could explain clearly how she felt she could no longer just *comply* and how the woman in the brochure who also resided in assisted living was taking a trip too. Of course, this wasn't a real woman, well, she was real, but, oh, things would get tangled if she tried to explain. And the letter in her purse had made her come to Chicago, though she wouldn't mention this to Sharon. Not yet.

Being surrounded by strangers made Betty inclined to reach out to someone, so she began talking with a woman next to her who was traveling south to see her sister as a birthday surprise. Betty confided that her own trip was also a surprise, an unauthorized trip from her assisted living apartment, and that she had business to attend to at a Chicago bank.

"I don't think I could put my mother in a *home*," the woman said. Betty flinched. Wicker wheelchairs, plaid lap robes, and tapioca pudding—the implied criticism of her daughter was too much.

"Oh, where I live has a computer room, library, spa, beauty shop." Betty waved her hand vaguely. "And a dining room, of course." A little exaggeration didn't hurt. This woman shouldn't think too badly of Sharon. "But it does get dull, and I wanted a little trip." Betty wrapped her arm more solidly around her purse handle, regretting her reference to the Chicago bank. The woman was a stranger after all, even though by now she had seen snapshots of the woman's dog and her sister in Tennessee.

"Won't your family be looking for you?"

"I don't think so. I left a note for my daughter." Actually, Sharon would be mad as a hornet to be left out of any decision, but the phone call later might smooth things out.

"You just be sure to have yourself a good time. You don't look like you need assisted living to me." The woman squeezed her arm in shared heartiness.

A red jacket caught Betty's eye, a red jacket with a black collar, just like Sharon's jacket. She gaped. It was Sharon's jacket with Sharon in it. And Vince was following behind her.

"Oh my God!" Betty exclaimed aloud for only the second or third time in her life.

"Is that them in the red coats?"

"My daughter and her husband." Sharon was striding ahead of Vince, jerking her head around like a chicken, for heaven's sake! Vince was trying to walk backward to look behind them. She wasn't kidnapped, just on a little train trip. Now how did they figure out to come here?

"You are so busted!"

"I'll never see the Sears Tower now! I'll be back in solitary at Shady Grove," Betty said, forgetting to sugarcoat her living arrangement.

"Yeah, I'd say your holiday is over. She's a pretty lady, looks a lot like you."

There they were, big as life. Betty and her companion watched as the red jackets made a second tour of the Grand Hall. Betty thought of the trouble she had put them through—hours of driving, the expense of gas, a Saturday lost—just to bring her home. She began to gather her things together. They would see her eventually, and she had better be cooperative. They would get out that silly step stool so that the old lady could get into the car (or was that thing a truck?), the old lady who caused so much trouble.

After a few more minutes, they seemed not to be looking for her. Vince put his arm around Sharon, handed her a tissue, and drew her over to a rack of brochures. Sharon put several in her pocket and together they examined another colorful flyer. Betty watched longer, this middle-aged woman and her husband, her Sharon driving all this way to find her. Betty loved her so much. How could she make it up to her daughter for causing all this worry, her Sharon Lynne who wanted the best for her and thought it was at Shady Grove?

"Looks to me like they're not so interested in you at the moment," said Betty's companion.

Sharon turned to Vince and smiled, something she didn't do often enough, Betty had thought lately. He put his arm back on her shoulder and kissed her. They stood together a moment, oblivious apparently to their errand. It was like a soap opera scene, with Betty and her companion rapt voyeurs.

"Might do them good to spend some time together," said Betty aloud. "She's either at work, doing something for me, or at her kitchen demonstration parties."

"Well, you know what they say, 'A wife's got to keep the home fires burning.'"

"Uh-huh," said Betty. "Sharon tends to everyone else's but her own. You know, I think I'll just slip outside for a few minutes. I want to see that Sears Tower."

"You do that. It's got a new name now, though it'll always be the Sears Tower to me. That couple's not going anywhere real soon. Go out that door over there and around the corner. You can't miss it."

Betty put on her jacket and stopped at the bag check area where she parked her extra handbag containing another sandwich and her rolling suitcase. She would have plenty of time to pick them up later, before her train, or, sadly, her ride back home with Sharon and Vince. Then she followed a sign for an exit.

She stepped outside into a glorious afternoon. Against the cloudless blue sky, the buildings looked like giant paper cutouts, with a bustling friendly scene at street level. She wasn't sure which direction to go, right or left. Her guidebook said the Sears Tower resembled an upright pack of cigarettes with several spilling out. Nothing nearby looked like that, so she headed toward the next corner, gripping her pocketbook. She could see a bridge ahead. Once on the bridge, she decided to cross the river and walk to the next corner.

She set one foot off the curb, but a taxi coming around the corner almost whisked her purse from her arm. The close call made her take another strategy of moving with other pedestrians. Soon some gathered at the curb, and she readied herself to move when they did. After a successful crossing, she checked her watch. With five hours until her departure, surely going along these streets was all right if she kept the station in sight. The Sears Tower had to be here somewhere! Sharon, Vince, and the bank letter were driven from her mind by the pulse of the city and her daring. She got to the end of the block and turned for the view, but still other buildings blocked the sightline. She turned another corner and met a crowd, whose noise had been covered by the traffic sounds.

A parade was coming—how fun! Why not delay her search for the Sears Tower for a few minutes to see the festivities? Soon the leading banner came close enough for her to see.

"Women's Rights are Human Rights." *Well, of course they are.*

Behind the banner came an assortment of women and a few men marching with many signs. Women in colorful saris or African dresses, a few in head scarves or dark robes, and many in jeans or running apparel, some pink, waved and chanted. Betty checked her pockets for something colorful and found a blue scarf to wave at the women carrying the sign "Celebrate the 19th Amendment: Vote!"

"I've never missed an election," she said to a woman next to her.

"Good for you, ma'am!" The woman gave her a thumbs-up that prompted Betty to give her scarf another flap toward the marchers.

In the old days, she and Charlie had gone to the polls together. They made a game of not telling their choices, but, of course, he expected her to follow his lead. After all, he was out in the world and knew what would be good for business and thus the country.

Several other signs indicated the enthusiasm for the election year: "Vote Like a Girl" That one was very clever, Betty thought. She'd have to tell Sharon, once they were on speaking terms again, or *if*. Well! They would patch it up sometime.

Mindful of the time, she tried to slip behind the crowd along the sidewalk, but the marchers were mixing into the crowd making it slow going. Apparently, this was the end of the route, and police began to appear along the fringes. More sign holders intermixed with the street crowds and Betty read avidly to keep up with the sentiments.

"End Child Marriage." *Of course marriage like that was wrong.*

"Equal Pay for Equal Work." *Well sure, but Charlie would have said women don't do the same work as men.*

Betty felt a tug and saw her blue scarf catch on the edge of a backpack. She tried to catch hold, but the scarf disappeared, bouncing along on its new perch. The signs dipped and swung as the carriers were funneled from the street to the sidewalks.

"Unborn Women Have Rights Too!" "We'll Remember in November." "MY WOMB IS NOT STATE PROPERTY!"

"A RAPE IS NEVER HER FAULT."

Should these things be screamed on the street? Betty wasn't sure this demonstration—yes, it was a demonstration, her first—was as nice as she had thought. Gone were the happy cadences and music. She felt pelted by the messages around her.

Betty tried again to get out of the crowd—she might miss the Sears Tower, but other people pushed in behind her to watch activity across the street where a group stood with signs and large photos. But of what? Betty moved forward to see. *Oh, fetuses!* The images surely were too tender to be bandied about on the street, with people yelling and shoving. A small flicker of panic grew about her aloneness in the crowd.

A woman pressed some colorful literature into her hand: "Give Girls More Than Plan B."

"Oh, I heard about it already," Betty said, hoping to connect with someone, but the woman was gone. Yes, the morning after pill—her bridge group had hashed that one out. "What will they think of next?" Ardyce had said.

Stuck in the crowd, she might as well see why people were gathering behind the sawhorses she hadn't noticed before. Only a small sign for a women's clinic on a door whose glass was covered with brown paper could be attracting attention. More people from the parade were gathering near the yellow barriers with their signs.

"Protect Women's Health!" "No More Back Alleys!"

The shouts reverberated on the buildings and the crowds pulled in tighter. As the signs jousted for positions, Betty gripped her purse tighter to her stomach and tried to take deep breaths to ward off the press of the crowd that was shoving her toward the curb. She had only seen things like this on the news, where such scenes belonged, she at a safe distance in her favorite chair with a cooling cup of coffee.

"Your choice isn't her choice!"

"Your body, your choice, your body, your choice!"

The chants rose in opposing rhythms, but this time Betty didn't want to join in. When suddenly she saw her mother in the profile of a woman nearby, the local scene dissolved as she thought of her girlhood. After the birth of her youngest sister, her mother had been slow to recover. Finally, after weeks in a darkened bedroom with the new baby, she rallied. The household returned to normal, with her father being good natured, teasing his wife and two older daughters. The raised voices she heard in the night she attributed to the usual farm troubles. Then a grown cousin had visited.

As she stood seventy years later on the sidewalk in Chicago, Betty could hear the women's voices plain as day. "Not another one! . . . Have you tried a very hot bath? . . . Vinegar and vodka? . . . I don't know what I'm going to do. . . . Over the bus station on the third floor."

Then her mother had taken an unusual overnight trip to town to stay with the cousin. Soon after, she had been feverish and weak. The cousin had returned to look after her for a few days, and finally, though her mother protested, the doctor had come. Betty assumed it was the expense of the house call that her mother feared. But now she understood.

Across the street, shades were lowered on the clinic windows, and evidently the door was locked, because if someone went out, someone inside unlocked and relocked the door for the unlucky patient who had to scurry through the crowd. Betty was only a few feet from a taxi that threw open a door to drop off a girl. In a short skirt and ripped net stockings, she was the sort of girl Betty was afraid of in the park, but this one looked terrified in spite of her spiked hair. When she stepped off the curb, someone tried to stop her, grabbing her arm.

People on the other side of the barriers yelled, "It's your right to visit a doctor!"

"Abortion is murder!" Betty turned to a woman next to her, surprised to see her yell at the girl, really just a teenager.

On impulse, Betty firmly took the girl's other arm and shoved the barricade aside. "Come on, I'll walk across with you. We can't let these people keep you away from your doctor, now can we?" The girl dipped her head, squeezing Betty's hand to her ribs.

They made their way to the opposite curb with Betty's purse swinging loosely as she marched smartly across the street. Hoots and calls came at them. Then people spilled out into the street, clustering around Betty and the girl. Cameras and reporters from a news truck entered the crowd, pressing microphones at Betty and her companion.

"Were you in the parade? Where are you from? Is this your granddaughter?"

Betty's heart pounded as she shoved by a shellacked-haired reporter. If this was a big heart attack, someone was around to call an ambulance. But she didn't think it was a heart attack of the medical sort, more like a weight of some sort lifting, something that had been there so long she didn't even know it was there. She was taking a stand. She gripped the girl more firmly as they made the final steps to the door, which was opened for them with hands reaching out.

"Thank you, ma'am," the girl said to Betty. "You be careful now."

"You be careful too, honey. Good luck." Betty hugged her and felt the girl press her cheek to hers as she made a rude gesture to the crowd then disappeared inside.

Betty felt someone grip her arm. "Right this way, ma'am."

"What?" It was a cop!

"Step this way." They walked her to a police van where several other people were being led, some willingly and some unwillingly. This was terrible! She must be under arrest, and for what? She hadn't even seen that Sears Tower yet.

"What's happening? Did I do something wrong?"

Betty had never even gotten a traffic ticket in her entire life. This was terrible but exciting too—*arrested*. She wondered whether she was losing her mind to think this way. Why, she didn't even have a lawyer to call since Charlie's had died last winter, so when she could make her one phone call—that's what happened on cop shows anyway— she would call Paul. That should liven up his day at Shady Grove!

"Am I arrested?" she asked the officer as he pointed to the open door of the van.

"You crossed a barricade, ma'am. Demonstrators are to stay within fifty feet of the clinic."

"A demonstrator?" Betty thought of Sharon with her kitchen gadgets. "Oh, but I wasn't, you know, demonstrating. I am on a See America rail trip. I just came out of the station to see the Sears Tower, and there was that poor girl with all those people yelling."

Any minute he would say, "Tell it to the judge, lady." She wondered if Judge Judy handled this sort of thing. Probably not.

Without a step stool, Betty clambered into the van, taking a seat beside a middle-aged woman still holding a sign. Betty wondered what the etiquette was about greeting people in a police van. Should she talk to these strangers? When was it that anything you said could be used against you? The policemen slammed the doors shut and the van took off, caroming around corners so that the passengers swayed back and forth. Betty caught glimpses of the tops of buildings. Perhaps one of them was the Sears Tower.

13
In Custody

Sharon and Vince wandered around the station but did not see Betty. They decided that the most likely place to find her was the Amtrak passengers' lounge, so they set up camp there. After many explanations, they were allowed in the first-class lounge too, but Sharon doubted that her mother would spring for an expensive sleeper. Vince went upstairs to get some sandwiches.

Sharon settled in the common lounge to watch the doors and look over the other passengers. Though Betty followed proper social decorum, she would strike up conversations with strangers, on occasion revealing personal details. Why were old people like that? She thought it possible that one of these waiting people had spoken with her mother. She considered asking for everyone's attention by clapping her hands or something, except people from trains from all over were here, not just the train that crossed Indiana. Instead, she would select some likely candidates who might have talked with or might remember an older woman. Passengers with preschoolers were a good bet, but most were obviously foreign, some not speaking English, some dressed in saris or other cultural garments, which would have discouraged her mother. The Amish party didn't seem likely, though she noticed one woman who was about her mother's age glance her way. Finally, she selected a neatly dressed senior citizen traveling alone.

"Excuse me, but I am looking for my mother." She approached the woman. "I am wondering if maybe she was on your train, or if you might have seen her here."

The woman shook her head and moved away before Sharon got halfway into her story. In the room were probably two hundred people, any of whom might have seen her mother. And tempers were beginning to run short. Continuous announcements alerted passengers on the southern-bound train of a three-hour delay in departure. The western incoming was also delayed. The western train outbound was on schedule and would depart in an hour, probably her mother's train. Mabel had hinted at the western destination after more cajoling and veiled threats. So where was Betty?

—m—

Upstairs Vince lingered in a sports bar where he ordered two hot dogs, Chicago style, for himself, though his heartburn might kick up. But they were in the Windy City after all, why not? He ordered a good-looking Philly steak for his wife and a coffee. Waiting for the food, he watched the big screen TV, some kind of late-breaking story about a demonstration. Elbow on the bar, he got interested in the close-ups of the screaming people. He was glad he and Sharon lived in a small city where people didn't carry on like this. He took a bite of one of his hot dogs, just a test case for the old gut, while he waited for Sharon's sandwich. With one hand guiding the hot dog and the other catching bright green relish as it squirted out, he saw what looked like his mother-in-law on the television.

"Violence broke out when someone who appeared to be a pro-choice supporter crossed police lines to escort a woman into the clinic."

In the scene demonstrators and cops poured into the street like hockey players, signs swinging. Vince shook his head. Something about the set of the woman's shoulders and the hair style looked very familiar. Vince put down his hot dog. *Could that have been Betty?* He started to pick up the sandwich bag to go tell Sharon, then sat down again. *This is nuts. How could it be Betty, who could hardly cross a street, let alone cross through a crowd of screaming people?* He would not upset Sharon with this bogus idea. She would go ballistic with worry if he told her this, and just when she was beginning to loosen up a bit, like her old self—Sharon before the tests at the fertility clinic years ago, Sharon before the kitchen gadgets.

Probably, right now, she had found Betty downstairs in the waiting room, and they would have to start back on the drive home through nighttime truck traffic. Just the thought of it made Vince sit down to finish his first hot dog, gut be damned.

—⁓—

Meanwhile, Betty was getting quite an education about civil disobedience. Her companions in the paddy wagon recommended she just tell the truth about her encounter and stress that she had not come to the city to join the protest. Another woman offered her a package of cheese crackers for fortification. They hashed over the current political climate surrounding *Roe v. Wade*.

"You know, I think my mother had one of those back alley abortions in the 1930s," Betty said suddenly. Her seatmates listened avidly while she aired her suspicions and the saga of her mother's continued ill health and early death from "women's troubles."

—m—

Meanwhile, Sharon and Vince ate the sandwich and hot dog, observing the other passengers and thinking about Betty.

"Does she have your cell phone number?" asked Vince.

"She said in her note that she would call us, but I don't know if she would think to call the cell phone or even have the number."

"Call the answering machine. See if there's anything there," Vince said, thinking about the woman on the news.

There were no messages. By the time they had finished eating, the train Betty presumably was going to catch was called. They watched every passenger walk through the gate. Betty was not among them. When the train pulled out, Sharon took Vince's hand.

"Now what?"

"Let's go over the facts," said Vince to repress the television news. "Your mother is in good health. She said she wanted a change of scene. Maybe she got here and decided to call an old friend or do some sightseeing."

"Maybe one of her school friends does live here," Sharon said doubtfully. "What I don't get is why didn't Mother just tell me this is what she wanted to do."

"Maybe she thought we would object, you know."

"Certainly, I would have," Sharon snapped. "She was adjusting well to assisted living last week. Now, she's gallivanting around the country."

"See what I mean? She felt like she had to take off without telling us," said Vince.

Well, if he wasn't going to tell Sharon about the TV news, they should stay around until tomorrow. The day was shot for working anyway. Maybe he could see the news spot again later without Sharon noticing.

"Since we're here, let's just stay over. I don't want to drive tonight," he said affably.

Sharon felt surprised at this suggestion but agreed when he pointed out they could check with the Amtrak agents in the morning to try to find out if Betty had changed her ticket. Maybe she would even be there booking a return on the eastern train to come home. Sharon got out a couple of honor cards for hotel chains and found accommodations in the Loop; they retrieved their bag from the car and walked out into the evening air. Vince pulled Sharon to the inside, like a gentleman, and she took his arm as they walked over a bridge. The tall, lighted buildings along Adams Street seemed watchful but not threatening as the couple threaded their way to their hotel downtown.

"This is turning out to be an expensive jaunt," Sharon said, thinking of the price quoted by the hotel. Irritation with her mother fought with worry over her whereabouts.

"Don't think about it now," said Vince. For someone who didn't like cities, he was warming to the flow of traffic and hurrying people, the sense of possibility conveyed.

Sharon pressed his arm with her fingers. Her mood was lifting. Hadn't she done everything right by her mother, as much as she possibly could?

"Maybe we should go out to eat after we find the hotel?" she said.

"Sounds good to me," he said. The hot dogs were hours ago now. He just had to be sure to catch some late news to watch for that peculiar story. With Sharon on his arm, he felt Dolly recede. Guiding her through the crowds, he had the feeling that he had Sharon's complete attention, well, other than what she devoted to worrying about Betty, but that was better than competing with kitchen gadgets and demonstration parties.

Betty was now getting an education in the results of civil disobedience at the Chicago Police Department. In fact, she was quite a celebrity since she was obviously the oldest of the demonstrators hauled in. Now the laborious process of booking the crowd was drawing to a close. Chat continued among her group and others waiting. Several asked Betty whether she would like to join their coalition that was planning on going to Washington on the anniversary of *Roe v. Wade*. As Betty listened to the women talk, she thought about her Sharon, how no doubt she had expected to have children. Betty had looked forward to being a grandma too. It was the proper ending role for her in the whole cycle.

By ten o'clock, the police had issued citations to some, given court dates to others, and let a few people off with just warnings.

Betty approached the sergeant when it was her turn and smoothed her jacket and grasped her purse. She had never been this close to a policeman before. Since he was black, she didn't think he was Irish.

"Name?"

"Elizabeth E. Miles."

He asked for ID. She could see he was both amused and annoyed with her. What was someone her age doing in a protest and now taking up police time, spending the public's money? Probably, he wished all these people had just stayed at home.

"When do I get my phone call?" Betty looked around at the green desks in the office. They certainly needed tidying up. They were strewn with coffee cups, hamburger wrappers, and a stray French fry or pizza slice. Uniformed people and those in street clothes worked at computers or phones.

"There's a phone right over there, Mrs. Miles. You can use it any time you want."

"Oh, I thought I would just get one phone call. If you commit a crime, I thought you get just one phone call. I want to call my friend Paul, a lawyer. He'll be very surprised to hear I'm in jail, instead of assisted living."

"I'm sure he would be, Mrs. Miles." The officer stopped typing to look her over. She hoped he noticed she was decently dressed in a suit. She moved her purse to her lap and wrapped her arms around it. Not everyone here looked like a nice person.

"You live in a nursing home?" The officer had dark circles under his eyes, and here she was, by accident of course, creating extra paperwork for him when out on the street were burglars and car thieves. And gangs selling drugs. She had heard all about Chicago's troubles on the news.

"Nursing home? Not yet. I live at Shady Grove where they do have a nursing home, but first you live in assisted living until you have a breakdown of some sort." Betty could see this man was much too young to have even thought of such a thing.

"I haven't had a breakdown yet," Betty said, "knock on wood." She leaned over and tapped the desk, only to find it was laminate. The officer crossed his hands on the desk and leaned forward.

"Mrs. Miles, protestors may not interfere with a legitimate business premises even if they disagree with the service."

"I wasn't protesting. I was trying to find the Sears Tower."

"Find it?"

"I went outside the station, but it must have been a back door because there was no Sears Tower, so I crossed the river and a couple of streets. I thought since it's so tall, you have to get back a-ways to find it overhead."

"As far as I know the Sears Tower—it's called the Willis Tower now by the way—is right where it's supposed to be."

"Well, I should hope so," said Betty. "I was just wanting to see it before getting on my train."

"You're supposed to be on a train, Mrs. Miles?"

This policeman was rather dense in Betty's opinion. Why else would someone be at Union Station? If he had this much trouble with interrogation, no wonder there were so many criminals on the loose.

"No, actually, I'm *supposed to be* at Shady Grove. I decided to take a train trip to see America instead of staying in assisted living where the only thing you see is yourself go downhill."

"Let me get this straight. You weren't here to demonstrate; you were just sightseeing, Mrs. Miles?"

"Yes, and then all those people were yelling at a girl who wanted to cross the street to go to a doctor's office." Betty noted that law enforcement, unlike the staff at Shady Grove, knew their manners enough to use her last name.

"So you walked across with her? You didn't notice the barricade?

"You mean those yellow sawhorses?"

"When you see those, Mrs. Miles, do not cross them next time, okay?" He waggled his finger at her. "We're going to let you off with a warning this time. You are free to go."

"Officer?"

"Yes, Mrs. Miles. Is there something else we can do for you?"

"If you run across my daughter and her husband, Sharon and Vince D'Angelo, they have on silly, red, matching jackets, tell them I'm on vacation." Of course, this was dumb to say, but it allowed her a few more seconds with this nice man.

"Sure, Mrs. Miles, it will be our little secret that you nearly ended up in Cook County Jail on your way to the Willis Tower."

Most of the other protestors had also been let off, and Betty found them standing together outside the police headquarters. Several knew each other and they laid plans for the trip to Washington. As the relief of being let go wore off, terrific fatigue set in and Betty tottered. Sharon and Vince would be gone by now, of course. If she ever saw them again, she would have to admit they were right. She was just too old for travel.

The women in the group waiting for cabs asked where she was headed.

"I was supposed to begin my See America tour tonight on the train. I guess my trip will have to wait until tomorrow." She looked around vaguely for Union Station. Such a large building was perhaps visible from here.

"Then you need to spend the night. But you don't have a hotel room, do you?" asked a woman about Sharon's age who introduced herself as Sara Weinberg. Betty agreed she didn't.

"We can't leave you on the street. You will come to my place for the night," said Sara. Betty felt alarmed. She couldn't possibly go home with a stranger in a strange city.

"It'll be good for my mother to have company, won't it?" Sara said to several of the others. "Maybe you can set her straight on a few things, Betty."

"Or she will set you straight. Sara's mother is a bad influence!" They laughed and waved goodbye.

"Oh, don't listen to them," Sara said. "My mother will be happy to meet you. She missed the parade today because she has a cold. Come on, we'll get a cab." Sara flung up her arm at a passing yellow streak and a taxi swerved to a stop.

Should she just go off with a stranger like this? Betty wondered. But she had nowhere else to go. She had no idea how to look for a hotel room in the city at night. Of course there weren't Holiday Inns just everywhere. So she accepted Sara's invitation, thinking *why not?* and took Sara's arm to be helped into the cab where she collapsed against the seat, too tired to feel afraid as the cab sped through yellow lights toward the address Sara had given.

14

The Kindness of Strangers

*A*fter ten minutes, they pulled up to a building on a busy, lighted street. A doorman appeared to greet them and press the elevator buttons. At first Betty thought it was a hotel with its hush-hush carpet, dark wood, and gilt trim, but she decided that this must be a condominium lobby. She explained again to Sara, who had insisted they use first names, that she had meant to be on the train tonight and not bothering anyone by being an overnight guest.

"Don't give it a second thought, Betty. We love company." They got off on the fifteenth floor, and Sara opened an imposing front door.

"Is that you back, finally? I thought you'd been arrested," a hoarse voice called.

"Not this time, Mother. I've brought us a houseguest."

"What? Don't mumble." Betty could hear the sound of slippers on the brown and black parquetry.

"Are you dressed?" Sara called out louder.

"Does she ask if my cold is better?" A cane tapped along and poked around the corner. "I could be dead and you wouldn't even ask."

"I said, I have a guest here," Sara said mildly.

"Oh. Do I know him already?" The slap of the slippers stopped.

"It's not a man, Mother. This is Betty Miles. I met her at the rally."

A short woman with oversized tortoiseshell glasses rounded the corner. "Well, for once it's not some starving artist you met at one of your groups."

She turned to Betty. "You should see who this daughter brings to her mother's house. It's enough to give a mother the big one." She pounded her heart.

"Puh-lease Mother," Sara said. "Which one of us has had three husbands?" But her voice was still light.

"The first two were just for practice! Now who is this Betty Miles?" She turned to face Betty, who knew she looked a sight. There was dirt along the hem of her blue skirt, and the jacket collar had gotten turned under somehow. She tried to rescue her coat that dragged from her arm.

Realizing this apartment, or should she say condo, belonged to Sara's mother, she felt she should apologize for her intrusion. "Sara was kind enough to invite me for the night, but with your cold, if you'd rather not have a guest, I understand. Perhaps you can direct me to a hotel?" Betty asked formally.

"Don't be ridiculous." The lady banged her cane on the floor. "Anyone who was at the parade is welcome, unless you're one of those self-satisfied hypocrites with an ass the size of Texas." She began to examine the potentially offend-ing area on Betty.

"Betty was on our side," Sara assured her mother, then turned to Betty. "Mother gets carried away. You'll have to excuse her language."

"Don't you tell me what to say, I'm not a child." She waved her cane at Sara. "My name is Eleanor Goldman, as my daughter failed to mention." She held out her hand to Betty and then continued, "Now where was I? Oh, yes. The worst ones you run into at these things are the young girls. What do they know about anything? Have they ever worked in the typing pool?"

"Well, maybe they—" Betty began.

"Whose asses do they think went on the line forty years ago to make sure they could do more than waggle their butts in the boardroom? Just tell me that?" She turned and glared at Betty.

"Mother, I'm sure Betty would agree with you. Just let her get a word in."

Eleanor, however, was off on a new topic. "You're prob-ably wondering why my daughter lives with me. I'll tell you. Because that no good husband of hers just took a job on the other side of the world in spite of her needing therapy. Now what kind of a husband is that?"

"Mother! That's enough." Finally, Sara was getting exas-perated. "You know Jake and I agreed it was best for him to go without me."

"No, he agreed this was the best way. If you had more balls, you would have said no."

"The way you did when Rudy wanted you to sell your business."

"Don't you go criticizing Rudy for that." She pounded the parquet with her cane. "At least I wasn't sick."

"I'm not *sick*," Sara said. "I do wish you would stop saying that. I just need a very common treatment."

Betty began to put her coat back on. "I really could find a hotel. If you'll just let me use your phone."

"You don't want to stay?" They both turned to her.

"I'm not sure you're in the mood for company."

"Us?" Sara said. "Oh, you mean the arguing?" She and her mother looked at each other and laughed.

"We'd love to have you," Eleanor said while grabbing Betty's coat. "Sara, take this into the guest room. What kind of hostess are you? Didn't I teach you anything?"

"You take her coat, Mother. It's your home. Remember? Let me just get out some supper."

Eleanor put Betty's coat in the closet and managed to get her to take off the blue suit jacket too, which she tossed on a chair.

Sara called from the kitchen. "Where's the bottle of brandy? I'm going to make coffee. And, sit down, Mother, so we can tell you all about the parade. Betty was quite the hero. She did nearly get us all arrested though."

"Really, damn this cold! It sounds as if I missed the best one yet."

The three of them gathered on a pretty loveseat and armchair in front of a gas fireplace, reaching often to a side table for the cheese-and-crackers plate and the brandy to lace their cups of coffee.

15
Other People's Beds

Sharon and Vince found their hotel and checked in. They were definitely more motel than hotel people and took in the artfully restored lobby before going upstairs. Though Vince wanted to watch TV news on various channels, he hoped he could engineer Sharon into a little romance. Here was a nice hotel room with a king-sized bed, something they didn't have at home. It was stacked with pillows, one curiously shaped like a sausage, and other apparatuses for love-making were nearby—a large bathtub, plenty of dazzlingly white towels, even terry robes, and little bottles of lotion and soap in the bathroom, as well as the large TV with pay-per-viewing. Could he persuade her for more expenditure along the line of an adult movie?

Perhaps a few of his old moves would put Sharon's fears for her mother on hold until the morning. It's not that that their marriage lacked sex, but too often at home his ardor cooled before release. Often, just as he emerged from a shower expecting a little *lovin'*, he would find Sharon upright in bed, fingering some complex kitchen tool meant for stripping a carrot or peeling fruit, its instruction booklet spread in her lap. Her passion for her business surely put a damper on impromptu romance.

Settling into their room, Sharon speculated again about Betty's whereabouts and decided she most likely had gotten on a train unnoticed. After all, maybe the elderly were boarded early or from a different gate.

Vince agreed, because even if his mother-in-law had been the woman on the news, she could have gotten on the train later. With her fears quieted again, Sharon began to enjoy the posh hotel room and stood at the window, looking out at the lights. Vince put his arms around her. His mustache brushed against her neck softy as he kissed her; he gently massaged her shoulders and neck as they stood mesmerized by red and white ribbons of traffic below them. He ran his hands under her sweater.

"Vince, we're in front of the window." He felt her lean in closer anyway.

"It's eighteen floors up."

"Look over there. We can see right in that window." Across the street, the windows, like television screens, displayed people engaged in various end-of-the day scenarios. Perhaps the view was as clear the other way of their room.

His massage continued more assertively and he felt her relax fully. Better not press his luck with an adult movie, he figured. Instead, he pulled the drapes and led her willingly to the bed. Even after all these years, Sharon was still a great lay, if he could just get her mind on him. Tonight, it just looked like he was going to get lucky.

An hour and a half later, Vince sat up rather abruptly, Sharon thought, and uncharacteristically said he wanted to watch the news. What difference did the news make to them, she thought, lying limply crosswise on the bed? Vince brought the terry robes from the bathroom and suggested she take a bath.

"Use all the hot water you want, why not?" he said. When the door closed, he began cruising the channels on the big screen. Maybe he could see that story about the demonstration again. Within minutes he did.

Damn! That *was* his mother-in-law, no doubt about it. This footage showed her from a different angle walking around a barricade with some girl on her arm. On two different stations he saw the demonstrators pile into the street behind the pair, with police following. Betty, who hardly ever expressed an opinion on anything, was out there defending a women's clinic. He just could not take it all in. He moved closer to the set to catch the audio, which he kept low.

"Police made arrests today when pro-life and pro-choice demonstrators clashed outside a women's clinic near Willis Tower."

Arrested! Did Betty need bail posted? Maybe she had called them at home, and here they had been in Union Station a few hundred feet away. There must be someone he could call to find out whether Betty was in custody. Maybe before Sharon got out of the tub he could use her cell phone to call the police. He turned her purse upside down on the bed. Sales receipts, coupons, a checkbook, keys, tissues, and a journal—*Sharon kept a journal?*—spilled out along with the phone. As he fumbled with the keypad, he remembered she could see calls made and received. He shoved everything back in the purse quickly, particularly the journal whose ragged edge cut his thumb.

"Vince, come try out this shower massage." Her voice was husky. Sharon didn't usually issue such invitations. Was she in the mood for more? Wondering if his mother-in-law was lined up with muggers in Cook County Jail had about done him in for a second round of romance. This was just his luck.

Well, he would try a quick call from the phone by the bed while Sharon had the water running. He could claim it was a mistake if it appeared on their bill. He pressed the concierge button to ask for a police number, mumbling something about needing to check on something he saw on the news. Surprisingly, within a few minutes, he discovered Betty was not in custody. What a relief. *But where was she?*

—∿—

About that time, Betty was still protesting, but weakly, against a third cup of coffee and brandy. The three women sat around the fireplace, their moods elevated considerably. Betty had been admiring the many antiques in the room, particularly a floral tea set with three cups and saucers.

"I don't know where the fourth cup went," commented Sara. "Do you know, Mother?"

"There have always only been three, far as I know."

"It's very pretty," Betty said again. "It seems to me I have seen that pattern before, but I'm not sure."

There was something familiar about the blue forget-me-nots on the cups and saucers. Betty had never cared especially for antiques. When she was first married, she felt relieved to leave the farm. Everything was so make-do there in her childhood; as a new bride she was glad to use blankets, not quilts, and to buy new furniture from the Sears store rather than accept the heavy oak pieces her father would have given her from the family collection. And, of course, she did have nice china and silver. People knew how to give appropriate wedding gifts back then. None of this making a bridal registry that included everything from smoke alarms to barbeque skewers. When the farm was auctioned finally, she did save some family pieces.

"Really, Mother, we've got to let Betty go to bed," Sara said long after midnight. "I'll see you both in the morning." Sara disappeared into one of the bedrooms and closed the door.

"I'm so glad I talked her into living here for a while. She starts radiation in a couple of days." Eleanor took Betty's arm to steady them on their way down the hall.

"She has cancer?" To Betty, Sara seemed much too self-assured to have cancer.

"They took out a lump a few weeks back on her breast. But she doesn't want to talk about it."

"Oh, I'm very sorry. You must be worried about her." The women faced each other.

"Yes, it's not right when it's your child and not you. There's something wrong with that. Of course, her doctor said we should be optimistic." Eleanor's bravado had evaporated, Betty noted. She wept quietly.

"I'm sure you have her in your prayers. I will too," Betty said.

"My prayers? You think the Universe is interested? You are an old-fashioned one, aren't you, Betty!"

Betty just smiled.

Then, looking Betty up and down while opening a door to a guest bedroom, Eleanor said, "Tomorrow we do something about that god-awful suit."

Laying her suit on her bedroom chair, Betty tried to picture what it would feel like to know Sharon had a terrible disease. Suddenly, she missed Sharon dreadfully. Maybe she should call to apologize for being difficult and promise to go home tomorrow and stay put at Shady Grove. But it was past midnight; there was no point in waking them up. This was not an emergency, and besides, she didn't know where they were anyway.

Tomorrow, she would call Sharon's cell phone, though now that she thought of it, the slip of pink paper with Sharon's cell number—the paper she was supposed to keep in her wallet—was tucked in the back of her address book at home. Once again, she had not followed her daughter's instructions.

Betty put on the nightgown Eleanor had leant her and settled into the high guest bed, which seemed dangerously near the window. She peered into the narrow street far below, then pulled the drapes, but she knew the drop-off was there, even so. Moving to the very edge of the bed away from the window, she fell asleep immediately.

—⁓—

In their hotel room, Sharon and Vince finally settled into the huge bed after Sharon had sat in the window again for a while. Any city always excited her. A city made her feel younger, as if her life weren't so set. She put aside her anger and worry over her mother and pulled the classy duvet up to her chin. There would be time for stress in the morning.

16

A Shopping Spree

ife began at a leisurely pace the next day in the condominium since they had all stayed up late, Betty discovered. She used the guest toiletries, counted her money, and put on her suit since she didn't have any wardrobe change. Then she sat on the chair by the window and took out her ticket to look at it. It was a scramble of poorly printed numbers, abbreviations, and codes in green and beige, though she could clearly make out her name at the top. It was exciting to hold something that promised so many possibilities. When Sharon was little, they had taken vacations in their station wagon—Washington, DC, Niagara Falls, and Mammoth Cave. But that was all long ago, of course. She took occasional trips with the senior citizen groups, but you just felt like cattle on those things. Get on the bus . . . sit here . . . eat this . . . use the restroom-now-because-you-can't-later. Everyone expected senior citizens to be so jolly, and sometimes the things they did were just plain dumb, like the kitchen band, clog dancing, or even the Red Hatters. Betty just couldn't see the point.

Of course, putting in time *was* the point, and what was the point of that?

Betty did not want to be a burden as a houseguest. Sara looked like the type of woman who had many places to go; perhaps she had a job too. Eleanor's cold might be better, and no doubt, she had activities to attend or friends to visit. Or maybe they had to grocery shop, though Betty wasn't sure how one did these chores from a high-rise. She hadn't seen anything like a grocery store or big box store as they drove through the streets.

More importantly, she had awakened full of remorse. Perhaps she was just a crazy old lady. Shady Grove would charge her for meals and laundry even when she wasn't there, Sharon would be hopping mad at not being consulted, and even Vince's good nature might be tried by her decision to come to the city. And she had nearly been arrested! She would never tell anyone about that little escapade. She should get over to the station and stay put until the returning train to Elkhart tonight. *No more funny business!*

Betty thought about phoning Sharon with an apology, but she was reluctant to place a long-distance call without asking. So she put her handbag on a chair near the door and went into the kitchen, thinking she could do up the cups and plates from last night. She had the sink full of suds when she saw a woman watching her from the door.

"Oh, you startled me," Betty said. "I thought I would just do these up for Eleanor." She wasn't sure who the woman was. She was in her thirties and dressed in slacks and a blue cotton top.

"Dishes are my job, ma'am. I'm Rosemary." Then she laughed. "I don't think Mrs. Goldman would wash a dish, even if there weren't any left. Here, you just let me finish."

"I'm sure I didn't mean to get in your way," said Betty. She knew people who had cleaning women but not household help. Then she introduced herself, though she wasn't sure if this was right either.

Betty wanted to get some juice or milk to take her pills, but she wasn't sure whether to ask Rosemary or get it herself. She edged toward the refrigerator.

"Can I get you something to drink, or how about coffee?" Rosemary began to set up a complex coffee maker.

"Could I have some juice so I can take these?" Betty held up a prescription bottle.

"Why sure. You know, Mrs. Goldman, she takes so many, we count them out in a box with times and days on them."

Rosemary got out juice and set the table. Betty admired the pretty placemats and bright-colored breakfast china she set out on a table by the window overlooking a park. In the distance, Betty could see Lake Michigan. She felt like she owed Rosemary an explanation for her presence.

"I just stayed for the night. Sara brought me back from the police station."

Rosemary seemed surprised.

"Well, I mean we got arrested together," Betty tried to clarify, then realized this was worse. Here she was telling family secrets to the help.

"Ms. Sara was arrested again?" Rosemary asked, shaking her head. "Sometime they're going to throw her in the slammer, and her lawyer won't be able to do a thing about it."

"I'm afraid it was my fault this time. If I hadn't stepped around the police sawhorses, maybe everyone else would have stayed on the sidewalk."

"Why, you're the lady I saw on the news!"

"I was on TV?" *Suppose this newscast went national. Suppose Sharon and Vince saw it! Could this be an embarrassment to Sharon at her job?* Betty pictured cascading events coast to coast giving Sharon more reason to think her mother belonged in a home.

"It was definitely you. You just stepped right into all those people with signs to lead that girl across the street," Rosemary said while loading the dishwasher. "It looked like nothing was going to stop you," she laughed. "You look like everybody's grandma."

"I'm not much of a joiner, and unfortunately, I'm not a grandmother either. But it didn't seem right that girl not being able to get to a doctor's office." Betty didn't go into her views on women's issues right then. But she had felt a monumental shift as she stood there in the crowd.

"I won't be here next week for Mrs. Goldman. I am going on vacation."

"How nice for you."

"It's the first vacation I've ever had where you go somewhere, not just to relatives." Betty recalled how that went, sleeping on couches and seeing slides of her husband's sister's trip to the Grand Canyon.

"Where are you going?"

"My boyfriend and I are going to Cozumel. Here, let me show you the picture of the resort." She shrugged in glee. "I show it to everyone."

Betty peered at the hotel brochure she had. It showed umbrellas on the beach with a handsome man holding a tray of drinks. "How nice."

"Yes, we're going to lie on the beach and eat out. I haven't put on a bathing suit in years. I got a new one, but I told my boyfriend, 'Don't expect miracles.'"

"I'm sure you will look terrific!" The woman's enthusiasm for her trip was catching as she showed Betty more photos, described her packing, and voiced her worries about flying.

"They say flying is the safest form of travel. Probably even more than rail," Betty said.

"Oh, but a train trip sounds so romantic, just like an old movie."

Betty was about to tell her about her own trip when they could hear Eleanor's cane tapping on the parquet. Betty hoped the late night had not made her cold worse.

"Rosemary, I'm ready for some coffee. Get it going!"

"Aye, aye, sir, I mean, ma'am," Rosemary pretended to salute as Eleanor rounded the archway into the kitchen.

Betty had prepared a little speech of thanks, but one look at Eleanor made her forget it. Instead of the bathrobe she was expecting to see, a hot orange-and-black print sweater over black pants with swishy legs steamed into the kitchen. A pink hat sat on top of her hair. Betty thought she looked like she was on fire.

Eleanor settled into the chair opposite Betty. "I have our day all planned," she said, twirling a diamond dinner ring.

Betty's composure returned and she began her recitation. "I have really appreciated all you and your daughter have done. It has been lovely to meet you all. Today, I really need to be on my way, if I could just make a long-distance call to my daughter."

Eleanor put down her cup. "You can leave me so soon? What do you possibly have to do today?"

"Well, my train ticket needs to be changed, and I need to call my daughter." She hoped Sharon and Vince were back home this morning. *Where they belonged!*

"What you need is another outfit. I don't think anything of mine would fit. I'm build like a fire hydrant—no hips, all chest, and you're more like a bowling pin, if you don't mind my saying." She pointed with her spoon. "Besides, that suit has got to go."

"Maybe it is rather mussed." Betty tried to smooth out the wrinkles.

"Mussed? Now tell me Betty, did you order that from one of those catalogs for sick people?"

Betty laughed. She got a number of catalogs and spent quite a bit of time comparing prices, styles, and so forth. Some featured easy-wear clothing with Velcro rather than buttons or zippers. "Well, it was from a catalog." This particular catalog had featured people still out and about, not in wheelchairs with smiling attendants on guard.

"Betty, it just screams nursing home."

Betty felt a bit hurt. She had bought this suit after much consideration two years ago. It was a practical color and promised to be wash and wear, and she had done both a lot. In winter, she added a snowflake pin to the lapel and wore a sweater under it. In spring, she could wear the jacket and not need her coat. An enameled bluebird replaced the snowflake pin. The suit came with both slacks and skirt; for city touring, she had chosen the skirt. This morning with Eleanor though, she felt like a grackle next to a parakeet.

"Come on, what we need is a shopping spree. Sara doesn't like me going out alone these days. She says I might fall. Well, I won't be alone, Betty, now will I?" She clicked off to her room, coming back with her purse and short pink jacket. Betty felt objections would appear ungrateful, and after perfect soft-boiled eggs, they went down the elevator.

At the entrance, Eleanor ordered the doorman to get her a cab and they were off. "Corner of State and Monroe," she said gaily.

The cab let them out right near the store Eleanor had in mind. Betty lingered, mesmerized by all the hurrying people and the noise. Boys played a staccato like a heart beat on overturned buckets across the street while a few feet away a pastor with a microphone addressed a congregation moving like a river: "Praise Jesus, people! Oh, Lord, we thank you for blessings!" Betty felt rooted to the sidewalk, afraid to cross the stream of people.

"Come on, Betty. We can look at the view later." Eleanor made her way through the revolving door with difficulty and faced an escalator inside the door. It didn't look like a department store to Betty.

Eleanor waved her cane and they started up, holding on to each other as they neared the top and taking little steps to carry them off the escalator. The view at the top was dizzying. Betty had never seen so many racks of clothes, piles of shoes, rows of handbags, sweaters, and scarves, and shoppers weighted down with merchandise.

"Now don't get taken in by the junk, Betty. Only look at the designer racks," ordered Eleanor as she led them

J o y c e   H i c k s

through the narrow aisles. Betty put out her hand to feel a polyester shirt, but Eleanor nudged her along.

"Not that, over here. We can't have you looking dowdy on your trip."

She planted Betty in front of resort wear, the trousers and knit tops in Florida colors.

"Now how about this?" She held out a jacket in pink and orange knit, printed in parrots.

"It's cheerful." Betty tried to find the right word for the jacket that looked at any moment ready to take flight. Next Eleanor held up a black-and-yellow striped sweater with black slacks. Betty would feel like a bumblebee! Eleanor forced it into her hands.

"Or nautical is always nice. Here's a light blue jacket and a red-and-white striped top with blue pants. How about that?"

Betty agreed this was more to her taste. Meanwhile Eleanor, working like a trooper, piled up a soft rose-colored running suit, a sequined shell, and a jacket that was printed with poodles. With plastic hangers sticking out every which-way, they could hardly make it to the dressing rooms, but Eleanor tap-tapped her way around, insisting to the sales-woman that they have dressing rooms next to each other and be able to take in more items than were ordinarily allowed.

"You think two old ladies are going to steal?" she said.

Betty had never tried on more than one or two outfits at any one time in a store, but the pile of booty made her feel reckless. She even put on the yellow and black outfit and agreed with Eleanor that it was very comfortable, if a bit startling. But she liked it and put it in what Eleanor called the "yes" pile. They decided the rose outfit was too light colored for travel. How about the poodles? By then, Betty had moved from objection to agreement. It was so much fun. Wouldn't Sharon be surprised to find her mother filling up a dressing room like a teenager?

"Listen, Betty, you need a new hat too, something for sun," Eleanor noted as they trudged out of the dressing rooms, arms full of the "yes" pile.

"Here, how about this one?" Betty took up a salad bowl–sized hat with the brim turned up, a floppy silk rose on the front. "I think the queen wore this one for Charles and Camilla's wedding." Betty, a devotee of the Royals, posed with her pocketbook held high, waving regally from the elbow.

"No, you look more like Dame Edna!" Eleanor screamed. Betty looked puzzled.

"That's a drag queen, Betty." Eleanor's eyes twinkled.

"A what? Oh, Eleanor!" They dove further into the pile of hats. Betty found a dark magenta one with a wide, beige brim.

"Here, this one's for you, Eleanor," Betty said, setting it on her shorter friend. "Oh, you look like a toadstool!" They fell on each other in hysterics.

Eleanor landed a white sailor hat on Betty's head. "Seriously, this might go with the blue suit." They both looked in the mirror. "No, I don't think so. Now you look simple." Betty agreed.

For a few minutes, their moods turned somber. Unlike the other clothes they tried on, the hats brought together too dramatically times past and those perhaps to come.

"Ooh, I'm afraid of landing in a nursing home drooling under a hat like that one," said Eleanor. "Just shoot me."

"It could happen, you know," said Betty. "Any time—a stroke, heart attack, collapsed lung. Do you ever think about that?" Her voice caught a bit. She supposed she was as brave as the next person, but she wondered how she would feel if she knew the end was in sight.

"I tell my children I'm going to live a very long time and be a problem to them all," Eleanor laughed. "So far, I've been right. I keep them on their toes."

"Do you come from a long-lived family? Did you take care of your parents?"

"My parents died in a concentration camp," Eleanor said.

"Oh, I'm so sorry. I didn't realize you are—" Betty stammered.

"Jewish? Yes. My sister and I had been sent to England, so we were saved."

"How lucky you were," Betty said, then sensed this wasn't the right response.

"Yes, of course, we were lucky. But you've never known anyone Jewish, have you, Betty?" Eleanor's lips were turned up on the edges with amusement.

"Not exactly as a friend, though of course I have heard that several people in the senior card group are. And they are lovely people, I'm sure." Betty felt she should say something more, but nothing Jewish about Elkhart came to mind.

Eleanor laughed. "Never mind, Betty. You're just getting yourself in deeper."

After the shopping expedition with so much exercise of trying on clothes, Eleanor suggested they ought to have lunch. Betty had put her clothing purchases on a credit card, and now made silent calculations of the cash she had with her and the budgeted funds for the trip in her checking account. She thought a sandwich in Chicago could be perhaps as much as ten dollars. She would get only soup. Surely, that would be less.

17

Men on the Loose

*E*leanor decided they should go to the Drake for lunch. Not recognizing the name of the grande dame of hotels just off North Michigan Avenue, Betty offered no resistance. When their taxi pulled up and imposing doormen ushered them into the lobby, the gargantuan urns of flowers, potted palms, and sumptuous rugs reminded her again that she was from Elkhart with only an Elkhart budget for lunch. Things might get awkward.

"I feel like a cocktail," Eleanor declared as they moved deeper into the lobby. "But first, we need to change our clothes."

"Here?"

"Certainly. There's a very nice ladies' restroom off the lobby. You can get out of that blue suit."

Betty knew she should be insulted by this remark, but Eleanor was having such a good time. Her friend meant no offense, and besides, Betty too was getting tired of the suit. After all, she was still Eleanor's guest. All these reasons made squirming in a stall through a change of clothes like a teenager, or sadder, a bag lady, acceptable. So when she reappeared in the yellow and black sweater and slacks, she felt like a new woman.

Eleanor led them to an elegant lobby sitting area where people were lounging under palms in deep armchairs with coffee, drinks, and tiered plates of sandwiches on low tables. A hearty commotion sounded as men in red and black appeared. At first, Betty thought it was a flood of hotel doormen.

"Oh my God, a Shriners' convention!" Eleanor clapped her hands. "Men on the loose, Betty. You'd better watch out!"

Other than when evading her neighbor, it had been quite a while since Betty felt she needed this caution. Yes, there were men at the senior center, but they were interested only in cards or pool. Most still had wives, and those who didn't generally took interest in the younger women. A few singles, as Betty and her friends said, were looking for a "nurse with a purse."

Betty had avoided any contact with men who looked in poor health. She had already done time with her own husband's heart problems. Besides, she still felt married and obeyed the conventions of fidelity. She felt she owed this to Sharon, who had been so fond of her father. Though one of her friends who had remarried reminded her that Charlie was not on an extended trip, she lived in a way that, should he reappear, she would have nothing to confess. She had kept only a few of his personal items, but she maintained their married lifestyle of restraint in everything. They had been cautious with their funds and generally content. Perhaps her upbringing on the farm had taught her that plenty one year did not promise it the next, no matter how hard one worked. Natural forces and chance must never be discounted.

Betty and Eleanor sank down in the comfortable chairs, joining the tableau of smartly dressed couples and groups of women scattered around. Soon the Shriners, in their red fezzes with silver insignia, dominated Betty and Eleanor's serious people watching. With their average age nearing seventy, the conventioneers spoke loudly, often pulling each other close to yell in an ear or shake hands. Betty's Charlie had been in the Elks, so she knew about men's secret societies. They had spent many Friday nights at fish fries, gone to occasional Valentine or New Year's Eve parties, and put in a lot of time at fund-raisers. Betty had been president of the ladies auxiliary for five years. Charlie had explained the various insignia to her—the red eye, the clock, and so on, as long as they weren't secret. Charlie had taken his membership seriously.

"Is that one the Grand High Mystic Ruler?" Eleanor pointed to a man with a particularly elaborate fez and other insignia.

"You're thinking of Ralph Kramden's lodge, the Raccoons, Eleanor," Betty said, poking her friend in the arm—she now thought of Eleanor not just as her hostess. "You know on that old show, *The Honeymooners*."

"Oh yes, with the raccoon-tail hats. Woo-woo," Eleanor imitated the lodge greeting of flapping the tail on the hat.

"Actually, the Shriners have a Grand High Potentate."

"You're kidding! Was your husband a Shriner?"

"No, my husband was an Elk. They have a Grand Exalted Ruler, but Charlie never got to be that."

"Well, we should definitely set our sights on a Grand High Potentate. Is there only one? I hope we don't fight over him," Eleanor declared. "Where's a server? I'm dying for a drink." She began to gesture toward the bar.

"There might be several retired potentates here," Betty said, thinking of the retired Grand Exalted Rulers she had known who attended events until the moment of death and even after at their elaborate funerals. She didn't often order a drink for herself and certainly not in the early afternoon. Also, it would cost a fortune here, but Eleanor spoke up when the server arrived.

"Two bloody Marys, lots of veggies."

Betty didn't have time to beg off and silently counted her cash. This probably reduced her to no dinner but that was all right, because she still had a peanut butter sandwich she could resurrect from her luggage at the station later.

The drink was a far cry from the plastic cup of tomato juice and vodka at the Elks. The large tumbler sprouted a complete stalk of celery hearts, tiny tomatoes on a toothpick, green pepper, and other things Betty couldn't identify. She gingerly approached the drink, trying to sit up high enough to get her lips over the rim. The noise at the other end of the room was getting louder, and a combo began to play big band music. The Shriners, some well oiled after a three-martini lunch, gathered near the musicians, back slapping and telling stories. A few took their wives to the dance floor, the silver tassels on their fezzes swaying as the couples dipped and swung.

"Come on, Betty, let's go over there," urged Eleanor. "I hardly ever hear live music anymore." Betty recognized most of the tunes—"Strangers in the Night," "Blue Moon," and "Impossible You." Maybe it was the alcohol, but it seemed the tunes were especially sweet, and carrying her drink, she followed Eleanor to chairs near the dance floor. She was glad she had changed out of her blue suit, wondering vaguely where she had left it.

They watched the dancers, rather than get lunch. Eleanor even sent requests to the band and got another round of drinks, in spite of Betty's protests. It was almost too loud to talk, so they just admired the crowd and tapped their fingers to the music. A couple of times Eleanor shouted, "Who's a Grand High Potentate?" She also engaged several seated gentlemen in conversation—the meaning of the saber insignia, the Arabic letters, and the Shriners hospitals. Really, she had quite a circle of admirers. Betty, amused by the obvious pleasure her friend took in the attention, wondered whether Eleanor was widowed, or lost husband no. 3 through divorce. Perhaps she would ask her later.

Plainly, Betty could see, some of the Shriners were getting downright obnoxious. Yes, this had been one of her objections to the Elks. Some people never knew when enough was enough, including Charlie. *Could an afternoon of drunkenness at a convention explain the lockbox?* Perhaps he had simply forgotten he put some Elks business papers there.

Betty glanced at her watch. Time remained to get to the bank. She could see now how to get around by taxi. Just name the place and the driver figured out the location. She had called to arrange for a ticket on the evening train west, but she still had to go to Union Station in plenty of time to pick it up and retrieve her baggage. So within an hour or so, she would have to leave.

The music, or perhaps the second drink, made her mind wander. She recalled the dances she and her sister would occasionally attend, without their father's knowledge since their church frowned on dancing. The farm boys hung around the edges of the dance floor watching the town boys cut the rug, swinging the girls and tossing their caps. Betty had loved swing dancing, with its fancy footwork and quick turns. Once she had even demonstrated her proficiency to Sharon, who immediately went to her room and slammed the door yelling, "That is really stupid!"

"Madam, would you like to dance?"

A portly man in a red fez stood in front of her. Betty was about to refuse but suddenly remembered Lathrop Higginbotham. In addition to his unfortunate last name, he had an extremely wide part that ran down the middle of his head and a pointed nose. Once, he had asked her to dance. She never forgot how he scuttled off when she refused. So something about the Shriner's sheepish look made Betty say, "Yes, thank you."

For a few minutes they merely stepped around the floor, each saying, "Excuse me." Then he took a stronger grip on Betty's upper body, and they moved into the music perfectly. Even in her sensible shoes, Betty found she could move into a fox-trot with the Shriner's hand guiding her. Not only was it delightful to move in time with the music, Betty took notice of the feeling of being in a man's arms again. Her back felt warm where his hand guided her with a slight pressure, turning them from side to side.

"Are you in Chicago for a visit, or do you live here?" he asked.

"I'm from Indiana, but I'm not really here for a visit."

He looked puzzled. It was difficult to explain why she was here. Should she mention she was a runaway and had been arrested? This would sound preposterous. He would think she was nuts.

"So you're here for the convention?" she said instead.

"I haven't missed a convention in thirty years, not a one." He guided them expertly around a couple planted in the middle of the dance floor just rocking back and forth. "I'm eighty-four and in perfect health, especially in the ticker." He pounded his chest. "In September I had bypass surgery and two valves replaced."

"You've made a good recovery then." Betty noted his healthy complexion.

"Let me tell you, it was touch and go for a while there. First, two days in the hospital before the surgery. My son took me to the emergency room, you know, and they wouldn't let me leave. Then they cut me open like a chicken." He let go of her hand to slice his chest. "There was a little hitch, so I was in intensive care for a week, full of tubes going in and out. You're only supposed to be there for a couple of days. They drained off a gallon of fluid out of my chest, my son tells me."

"Ah," said Betty, hoping to concentrate on the music.

"Then after three more weeks in the hospital, I went to a rehab place since I live alone. Stayed there for six weeks, sitting around waiting for fluid to drain. Let me tell you, that fluid's the clinker." He leaned Betty into a slide and dip. "Turns a man's nuts into a sack of potatoes."

"How many people did you say are at this convention?" Betty shouted in his ear.

"About two thousand. Well, like I was saying, they put pig valves in me. Did you know that's how they do it?" He spun her around.

"Yes, it's remarkable." Betty began to look for Eleanor.

"First they tell you don't eat sausage or bacon for your cholesterol, then they use a pig valve," the Shriner went on. "It's not a pretty scar." He touched his chest.

"I suppose not," Betty said, determined to look only over his shoulder. She had heard a dozen of these heart surgery stories and been shown a few scars. Men were so happy to wake up alive, they wanted to take everyone else along down memory lane. That David Letterman on TV, for example. It was years before he could get though a show without mentioning his heart surgery.

"Have you thought of moving to a retirement place or assisted living?" Betty tried to steer them to a topic that worked every time with senior citizens.

"Not me, not with my ticker all fixed up." Why discourage him with all the tales she knew of men who made subsequent hospital trips for strokes, stents, clots, and so forth?

Several other couples gave up on the small dance floor, leaving the space to Betty and the Shriner and two other couples. Betty had forgotten how much she liked dancing. She and Charlie had even taken Arthur Murray dance lessons at one point.

After several numbers, Betty thanked him.

"No, I owe you thanks," he said and took out his handkerchief. "My wife passed only last year. We had been married for fifty-three years." He got out his wallet to take out a photo.

"I'm so sorry. You must miss her. What a pretty woman." Betty peered at a photo that must have been thirty years old.

"Yes. Nothing is the same," he said, putting the handkerchief to his lips.

"It does take time getting used to being alone."

"You lost your husband too?" His hopeful tone sent up a red flag.

Betty explained that it been a number of years ago, but still she missed him, though time did heal, of course.

"I appreciated dancing with you," he said again. "I just miss having a woman around." He wiped tears off his face, begging her to excuse his breakdown. He still gripped her hand. "How about dinner?"

Unlike some of the Shriners, Betty knew when enough was enough. She could see he was already picturing her doing the tremendous pile of laundry that collected in the closet and mending the hole in his pants pocket where his keys fell through.

"It was nice to dance. Thanks very much. You go and find your friends now." Betty steered him gently toward a group of men near the bar, then returned to Eleanor.

"Well, he wasn't a Grand Potentate, but was he potent?" Eleanor said as Betty sat down.

"I was afraid I'd find out at any minute. He seemed ready for show-and-tell of his chest scar, at least." Betty giggled.

"Oh, they're the worst kind. And I hear with this Viagra, they think they're still Niagara." Eleanor made hand gestures, while Betty tried to look disapproving.

"Seriously, Betty, from what my friends say, that stuff is quite popular in retirement communities."

"Well, I should hope not in assisted living."

"Maybe you'd better say, you should hope so," retorted Eleanor who quickly went from hoarse laughter to a coughing fit. She pressed her hand to her chest and tried to wave Betty off who patted her back tentatively. The choking passed, but Eleanor now was flushed and her breath seemed shallow. She leaned heavily on Betty as they walked toward the lobby where they picked up their shopping bags from a bellman. Then they hobbled through the main doors to the street. Betty motioned to an elegant doorman. "Cab, please." He blew his whistle and waved grandly at the taxi line. Eleanor began a wheezy cough again.

"You go right ahead, Betty, and get another cab for the station. I'll be fine," she gasped. The doorman held the cab door open and handed Eleanor in, but she looked very fragile and now pale, hunched in the back seat. Betty glanced at her watch to calculate the time she needed for the bank, her baggage and ticket, and going through the maze of the station. Then, of course, there was the call to Sharon. *Well*, she thought, *whatever will be, will be. How did that French phrase go? Que sera, sera.* She got into the cab next to her friend and patted her hand.

"I couldn't possibly leave without knowing you got home safely," she said.

"Thank you so much," Eleanor wheezed. "Now you can stay with us another night." Her eyes twinkled. *Had the cough*, Betty wondered, *been manufactured for this purpose?* Eleanor's flush and later pallor seemed legitimate, however, and Betty settled back in the seat after giving the driver Eleanor's address.

—⚍—

Early that morning, Sharon had woken up next to Vince in their $275-a-night hotel room thinking of death. A conversation had come to her mind, one she had had with her mother years ago, shortly after Betty's father had died. Sharon had been only about ten. She went into the kitchen, finding her mother in tears and sniffling. Some girls would have offered comfort, but she clearly recalled she had stood aloof and embarrassed, just inside the door. Her mother was not usually one for tears. Betty had said, "I'm thinking of Papa."

"But he was very sick." Sharon recalled her irritation with all the tedious phone calls between her mother and her aunts, fussing about how to take care of him. At the end, none of them had cried at the funeral.

"Yes, of course, no one could make him better," her mother had said, and then gone on, "but losing a parent is a milestone." Her mother had looked at her levelly. "When your parents die, it makes you realize that you're really next."

Sharon supposed she remembered this conversation because it was so unlike her mother. Usually her mother asked about Sharon's friends, her homework, or her next Girl Scout project. It had frightened her to have her mother suddenly address her as if she were a person, not a girl, not a daughter. Even more surprising, her mother had turned to her and said, "Do you ever think how you will die too someday?"

She had said "No!" and lied that she had to go to the library for an assignment.

This was the only time they had ever talked about death in this way, only that one time in all of Sharon's life. The subject of personal mortality had not even come up when her own father had died after several months of congestive heart failure, though she had been devastated. After she and her mother had made all the proper arrangements, her mother had slipped into widowhood without drama, and Sharon had done all the right things—helped her mother sell the big house and move into a duplex, did her income taxes, took her on outings, and finally moved her to Shady Grove.

Now, lying in bed hearing traffic and Vince's snores, she felt her heart pound as an intrusive thought struck her.

Could my mother be dead?

They did have some affinity. Often when Sharon called her mother, Betty would say, "Why, the phone didn't even ring. I just picked it up to call you, and here you are!" On occasion, Sharon would feel prompted to put some odd item at the store into her cart to give her mother—aluminum foil or shortbread cookies. When she handed over the goods to her mother, Betty would say, "I just put that on my shopping list."

Yes, it seemed to her that some essential cord would feel broken if Betty were dead. Sharon closed her eyes, searching around, as it were, for a missing piece, but nothing seemed out of place. No empty slots on any shelves. Suddenly irritation bloomed. Here she was in a beautiful hotel room with Vince for once, and she had morbid thoughts and even selfish ones, she had to admit. Maybe her desire for her mother to be safe and sound at Shady Grove was just an act of self-preservation in the end. As long as you had one living parent, you weren't next.

Vince turned over awake. "How'd you sleep?" he rubbed her shoulder. He had slept like a log—he couldn't remember a night so seamless.

"Okay, I guess." Sharon kept her daydream to herself. Vince was somewhat put off by that sort of talk, and now that she was fully awake such ideas seemed counterproductive since they did not suggest a plan of action.

"Now what do we do, Vince?"

He was a little surprised since Sharon rarely was at a loss for making a decision. "Where could Mother be?" She flipped on the TV. "Why would Mother do something like this? Why does she want to drive me crazy? If only Daddy had lived longer to keep her company."

She paused on the internal hotel channel looking at the breakfast menu—egg scrambled with spinach and pesto, marbled toast and marmalade. Sharon considered the marmalade, an interesting idea paired with pesto.

"She is so unfocused alone. Have you noticed how her mind wanders? Why, the other day she asked me if I thought her friend Mabel might be a lesbian! Look here, Vince, juice and a muffin is ten dollars. Think how much just the room is costing us."

The channels rolled past cartoons, prayer line, yoga, home makeover, adult movies (Vince paused hopefully on his way to the bathroom). Sharon halted at a local morning show. *Suppose that some newsclip about the demonstration was on?* Vince grabbed the remote and pretended to be interested in a program on fly-fishing. Even though he knew Betty was free, he would be guilty as charged for withholding this evidence of her evening whereabouts.

"How about breakfast and a look around, as long as we're here?" he said. And get away from televisions, he was thinking.

"What about that finish-up you said you had at that beauty shop tonight? Don't you want to get back?"

"That can wait," he said vaguely, grabbing his pants and shirt. On the one hand, they were certainly running up bills, but on the other, putting distance between himself and Dolly made him feel easier. He could just as well check on the water heater when the shop was open.

—ᴥ—

Out on the street, Sharon felt her mood lighten. So what if breakfast cost as much as dinner at home? Didn't she deserve to have a bit of pleasure, what with a difficult mother? Probably Betty would head back home today, frightened and remorseful. She would apologize for causing them worry. She would thank them for helping her make the decision to move to Shady Grove where she would be safe. Her message would be on the home answering machine later today, Sharon was sure, but she wanted to check around Union Station again, so they headed over the Adams Street bridge, pausing to watch a mallard family and a kayaker. Descending the escalators to the lower level by Amtrak, she checked all the ladies' rooms, had her mother paged, and again tried to extract information from ticket agents. But this was a hopeless enterprise—which agent in the line of personnel might have served Betty? She talked to several, but brusque or folksy, no one could say they had seen her mother, nor would they confirm whether she had a reservation. And by noon, no new messages were on the answering machine at home.

The couple sat down on a bench in the grand waiting room. Sharon's spirits had plummeted, her optimism and self-righteousness evaporated. She put her head on her husband's shoulder. "How could I let this happen? What will people at work say when they hear something terrible has happened to my mother."

"It's only been one day."

She was surprised to feel tears coming as she thought of her mother—small and in her blue suit—in the big city. "A lot can happen in twenty-four hours, Vince."

He agreed with that—both good and bad—but he didn't say so. "Sure, but let's not get too worked up yet."

He tried to pat her hand. He knew it was a bad sign that she was crying, rather than organizing them. "How about we come back here this afternoon about five for the trains. She may have had her lark and be ready to go home." Privately, he thought the demonstration would have cooled her jets. "Come on, honey, can you cheer up a little? You said we should have a vacation."

Sharon wanted to rant at him that she had meant a planned vacation where you tell your coworkers, mark your calendar, and debate over what to pack, but she was too worn out. Maybe this surprise twenty-four hours in the city was all she deserved, and she had better make the best of it.

They stepped back outside into a lovely day. Sharon chattered about the tour boats on the river, the planters of tulips, the way the clouds were reflected in the glass towers—wasn't it beautiful? Vince glanced apprehensively at the Willis Tower rearing above them. He swallowed, his hands gripping the linings of his pockets. He knew Sharon would like to go to the top, but he just couldn't. A pretty woman walking toward them sauntered along on shoes like the kind Dolly wore, slingbacks, she had told him. He glanced a bit too long. The woman smiled and nodded slightly. Temptation was everywhere.

"Want to visit the Willis Tower, honey?" He transferred his gaze to the charcoal monolith.

"Vince, you hate heights."

"Long as we're here, we might as well play tourist." He threw an arm around Sharon.

"You think you'll be okay? You sure it won't bother you?" Sharon tipped her head way back to look up. "We don't have to, you know. We can just look at the lobby." He noticed she had begun to use her work tone of voice reserved for difficult situations.

"I'll be fine."

He concentrated on how much it would please her. As they entered the lobby, he looked around at the tourists. Other guys like him were lining up. It must be okay. He would be okay. His spirits flagged at the security measures, as if he weren't thinking of 9/11 enough without passing through metal detectors, opening Sharon's purse, and sitting for security photos taken against a photomural that simulated a ledge over the skyline.

On the other hand, Sharon's spirits rose. It wasn't often they did a tourist attraction, and she wondered why Vince had suggested this one in particular given his fear of heights. On the elevator, Vince concentrated on watching some kids. Even though he might deserve punishment, surely God would protect these children. The elevator would make it.

He took some deep breaths, quietly forcing himself to let them out slowly. Sharon squeezed his arm.

They stepped out of the elevator to blinding sunlight, as if the doors opened to heaven itself. Sharon burst into tears.

"Oh, Vince, I just thought. Mother always said she wanted to visit the Sears Tower. I never would take the time to bring her here. I put it off so long, now it's got a new name."

Was this more punishment for him? He had gotten to the top and now she was in tears. Vince gestured around vaguely. "Maybe she was here yesterday, honey." He found a napkin in his pocket and handed it to her.

"Or maybe she's on her way here today. I hadn't thought 'til now! This is the one place she would come. We can just sit down and wait." Sharon headed them toward a bench facing the view. Vince sat on the edge of the seat and looked at his shoes, then mumbled that he was going to the men's room.

Thankfully, near the restrooms were some benches where he could face a soft grey wall of vintage photos of the city. "You just look around," he called out to his wife. "I'll be right here."

She looked enviously at the couples hand in hand and at those daring each other to step into the glass cube overlooks. For heaven's sake, she deserved some break from her worries. Vince was tiresome on occasions with his height thing. He should just relax and enjoy the views like other people. Then she remembered they weren't like other people. She was a woman whose mother had run away from her.

She looked out at how the streets were laid out below, everything neat and organized and predictable from up here; every street appeared to lead to a known destination, though distant. When you were down below, patterns dissolved, pathways lacked rhyme or reason, leading you to places at random—like her choosing Vince, for instance, who could give her no children. But how could she have known? Only someone with a bird's-eye view, like God maybe, could have predicted the results and recommended a different route. On the ground, you just chose without the privilege of that overview. And would she have chosen differently? She glanced over at Vince hunched up, looking at his shoes. For sure, he was visiting the Willis Tower just for her. No, she would have chosen him anyway.

"You ready to go, Vincie? We've seen it, I think." She took his arm, and he pressed her hand to his side, as if she might jump off.

"Mother would love this. I hope she got here before, well, I just hope she gets here," Sharon finished up.

In the elevator a club of Red Hat women were joking to one in purple. *It must be her birthday*, thought Sharon.

"You think if we drop fast enough, I'll go back to being seventy-five?" said the one in purple. "Like a time warp?"

"We zoom any faster, your boobies are going to be back where they belong," said another.

"Elsie! There's a man present." She gestured at Vince. "He's going to get embarrassed."

Vince laughed, but he wondered whether he would make it to seventy-five if he had to go up the Hancock building too. Sharon watched the women, and for the third time that day, her eyes filled. These women were out having fun. Where was her mother? *Under a bridge? In a hospital?* She made a vow. If she ever found her mother, she would make sure she had fun, and lots of it. She would be a good daughter, even if it killed her and her mother both.

—⁓—

More hours combing through Union Station, badgering Amtrak personnel proved fruitless. The demonstration news was old news, and Vince convinced himself it was okay not to mention this to Sharon, but he had uncharacteristic patience with killing time. Since it was hours before the next Amtrak departure west, they walked back to State Street in the late afternoon, encountering a small crowd on the sidewalk. Inside the huge windows, TV anchors were broadcasting the news, which was piped to the street. Large screens played the various news footage, weather, and so forth. Sharon and Vince paused. It was fun to watch anchors in person whom they usually saw on-screen in their den

"Fancy dress was the order of the day at the Drake this afternoon where the Shriners are in town for their national convention," noted one anchor.

"Vince, look there," Sharon shoved aside people to get to the window. "That looks like . . . why, that's Mother!" Sharon exclaimed, pointing to a lady in a yellow and black sweater dipping as her partner led her in a fox-trot.

The other anchor chirped, "There's a move you don't see much these days! Looks like the tea dance was a popular event with the ladies."

"What's she doing?"

"Dancing, looks like!" Vince ventured.

"But who is that man? Where is this?" Sharon put her hands on the glass and gestured to the anchors before Vince took her arm.

"They said the Drake Hotel."

"Let's go right over there. The Shriners! All the drinking and men."

"Honey, your dad was an Elk. I'm sure she's fine."

"Oh, yes, I remember the Elks all right! Get us a cab!"

Long beyond worrying about money, Vince booked a room in the Drake while his wife staked out the lobby. *A lavish room and bathroom again tonight, perhaps with sex to match,* Vince ruminated as he wandered around, his sneakers clumsy in the deep pile of crimson carpets. He took in the smartly dressed, pretty women at high tea among the potted palms in the lounge, contrasting steeply with the few lumpish Shriners left in the lobby, fezzes askew. Sharon wandered along the corridors of the meeting rooms, asked for Betty at the reservation desk on the slim chance that Betty had checked in, and interrogated the concierge about four feet from where her mother's blue suit lay, tangled and unnoticed, in the lost and found at the bellman's station.

No one could particularly recall seeing a woman with grey hair—rather frail and perhaps confused. No, they couldn't say positively. This left husband and wife with another night to kill in an elegant room with a lake view. Sharon felt she owed Vince for the Willis Tower. Vince worked hard to keep her mind off her mother.

18

Priceless Art, Private Revelations

"Betty, if you don't get on that train for your trip to-night, you never will," Eleanor said the next morning, an echo of Betty's thoughts. They were in the guest room where Betty was gathering her things.

"Yes, I may lose my nerve." It had seemed so right before to go West. Glancing at the phone, she realized that she still hadn't called Sharon. Once delayed, the call seemed impossible.

"Don't you dare put on that blue suit again." Eleanor fussed with Betty's new outfits, laying out possible combinations.

"I can't. We left it at the Drake." Betty kept a straight face with difficulty.

Eleanor picked up the receiver of a bedside phone. "Should I call to ask? 'Concierge, my dear friend took off her blue *Chanel* suit and left it in the ladies' room. Be an old sport, and go to look in stall three.'"

They laughed, poking each other and embellishing the imagined call and the response of the haughty hotel personnel. Eleanor sat on the bed to supervise the packing of the new outfits into a paisley cloth bag that she insisted Betty take. While Eleanor folded, Betty opened each purse compartment twice, fingering carefully through the internal pockets.

Last night she had had quite an upset when she couldn't find the bank letter. Perhaps it had fallen out either during the shopping or the cocktails, one more incident speaking to the foolishness of her actions. Charlie had complained about the messiness of her personal belongings; here was proof of her failings. In desperation, she had tipped out the contents of the purse onto the bed, but the panic was only a veneer over the realization that, with the blasted letter gone, she could just forget the whole lockbox thing. However, one more pawing through the jumble revealed the letter had just become tangled with the notebook, following her like toilet tissue stuck to a shoe and equally unwelcome.

"What have you got in there, Betty?" Eleanor said after watching Betty check through her purse for the third time. "Only the Queen Mother has a pocketbook like that anymore."

"And she's dead!" the two whooped.

Betty snapped the clasp open and closed twice more. "Let me ask you something, Eleanor. What would a man keep in a safe deposit box?"

"Money, stock certificates, a new will, or a private peccadillo—like a jar of toenail clippings, for instance. Why do you ask?" Eleanor patted the bed for Betty to sit.

"How about a box his wife didn't know about?"

Betty went on to describe the letter and the mystery of Charlie never having mentioned the safe deposit box to her. He only went to Chicago to the company headquarters a couple of times a year. What use could a safe deposit box be in Chicago when they had one at their own bank at home?

After Eleanor described similar foibles of old acquaintances, they debated over possible contents of Charlie's box, good and bad.

"What it boils down to, Betty, is whether you really want to know what's in there."

"I'm sure my Charlie had nothing to hide."

Betty grabbed the blue and white nautical sweater to refold, though Eleanor had just tucked it neatly in the bag. This woman who had had three husbands had nerve suggesting that her one husband may have had faults. Why, they had celebrated their fifty-seventh anniversary right before his death. She went on, "But I guess I'm not so sure, or I'd have gone to the bank first thing when I got here."

"So, why did you put it off?"

Because something in a lockbox could change everything. You want reassurance that your vision of the world was without cracks, that the guidelines you had lived by had been set by a moral compass based on true north, that you had chosen the *right way*, even when sometimes you could see other ways that looked tempting.

Betty shrugged. "You know what they say. 'Let sleeping dogs lie.'" The blue and white sweater got another folding.

"Are you going to live the rest of your life stuck in adages? You're far from dead yet, Betty! Find out what's in there. Find out if he was a prince or a prick! I, for one, want to know!"

"Eleanor, really!" Betty removed from the bag an orange scarf Sara had pressed on her earlier.

"What I'm saying is you seem to have had a good life with one husband and a daughter. You should find out the whole picture of that life, not be afraid of some possible wrinkles in it."

Like the photo with the raised eyebrow—Betty pictured it trapped forever in assisted living under her placemats.

"I guess I should just go right to this bank."

"Or at least call. Maybe they would send the box contents to you." Together they refolded the scarf, putting it back in the bag along with the nautical sweater.

Bank management said she would be required to mail or fax various forms, identification, and a death certificate before the contents could be shipped at her cost. Instead, she set an appointment for late in the afternoon.

They decided Betty would have to amuse herself alone until her appointment and even later train, since Eleanor wanted to accompany her daughter to the hospital for her first radiation treatment. But this would not be a final parting, since Eleanor had made Betty promise to visit her at her time-share in Florida next winter and come back to Chicago sometime in September. Eleanor recommended that Betty should go to the Art Institute. This was someplace she could spend the better part of the day, find a safe place to sit down and rest, and eat her lunch. Betty felt she didn't know much about art, well, real art, the kind in a museum.

"What's to know? Just go in and look," Eleanor retorted when Betty expressed her ignorance.

"Of course, there is some art in Elkhart." Betty decided she should defend her hometown but wasn't sure the paintings displayed at the senior center or her dentist's office really classified as art. There were some small shops selling photographs, pottery, and a few other things, but she had rarely been in them. It was too awkward to say, "Just looking."

—◊◊◊—

During Eleanor and Betty's planning session in the Lake Shore Drive condominium, Sharon and Vince, only a few blocks away, sat down in the Drake Hotel restaurant for a leisurely breakfast. Feeling magnanimous of any of his faults, Sharon let warmth for her husband overshadow anxiety over her mother and agreed they should have the buffet breakfast in spite of nearby fast food. As they strolled around the buffet stations—fruit, cereals, baked goods, smoked salmon, sliced ham, and the hot dishes—Vince pointed out that the carved watermelon fruit basket lacked the lattice edge that Sharon put on her version. The pineapple looked like a porcupine, not a flower, they observed, with its prickling of tooth-picked cherries. They filled their plates slowly.

"Look, honey, watch the omelet guy." Sharon nudged Vince.

"Yeah, it's all in the wrist."

"But yours flip twice."

"I've got twenty years experience on him, though." And some very expensive cookware that Sharon had collected through her success with the home demonstration parties.

They ate slowly and refilled twice to sample anything unusual. Sharon touched on a favorite topic—how she'd like to start a catering business. They covered the negatives: no health insurance if she quit at the hospital, their need for a loan, riskiness, and so on. She sighed and Vince said, "Maybe someday."

Then they laid out a plan for the day—ambling through stores along North Michigan Avenue—agreeing that if Betty were not at the station tonight and left no messages on the phone, they should go home to wait. Sharon said she would call the police to ask about filing a missing person's report if they had no news.

—ᴡ—

Meanwhile as Vince ate his last bacon strip, fifteen blocks south on Michigan Avenue, Betty inched her way out of a taxi right in front of the imposing Art Institute. Breathless when she got to the top of the steps between the lions, she turned to admire the view, a wonderful panorama. At her feet lay one of the most famous streets in the world, Michigan Avenue, with its river of humanity. And here she was, Betty Miles, going to spend her day in the heart of culture, in one of the world's best museums. *If only Sharon could see me now!* She hoisted the paisley bag to her shoulder, gripped her purse, and headed inside.

Thank goodness they had a place to check her bag. She marveled to think how her belongings were scattered around the city—her new outfits here, her blue suit tossed out at the Drake Hotel, her hat left on Amtrak, and her larger suitcase checked at Union Station. Three days ago, this would have caused her great anxiety. Today, she could care less. The stuff was replaceable.

She took the brochures offered where she paid an entrance donation—rather pricey, but Eleanor had assured her it would be worth it. Where to begin? Greek, Japanese, Chinese, Renaissance, modern American? With a long flight of stairs in view, she decided to just look at whatever was there when she got off an elevator she saw on her left. She followed some other people on and off.

Eleanor was right. All you had to do was look. She wandered through religious pictures. It was like a roomful of large Christmas and Easter cards, except for the martyrs, of course. She quickly passed a couple of fellows bristling with arrows but stopped to look reverently at the Madonnas. Even though they looked like paper dolls taped in the frames, she liked their faces. Astonishment, fear, joy, and sorrow—the basics of motherhood!

Betty wandered through some other galleries looking at dozens of pictures. Some were silly—Cézanne's *The Bathers*, for example. Betty sat down to look at this one—the foamy turquoise background suggesting sky and water was a pretty color, and green brush strokes made leafy trees. In the foreground about a dozen nude women divided into two groups were in different stages of bathing outdoors. This was one of a dozen on this subject she had seen already! Only once in the locker room at the Y had Betty seen women in such naked community. Polishing their big bottoms with greyish towels before stepping into cotton panties, the Silver Swimmers had nattered easily about ordering shoes online and a new turkey chili recipe. Betty had washed her hands and hurried out.

Cézanne's women, also in very ample proportions, were drying off, leaning over, combing their hair, and bathing their children. The figures were indistinct, but she could see some women were in the water, some reclining on their stomachs, some leaning on each other. She walked up close and the figures dissolved into peach, blues, and greens. Stepping away again, she saw the figures move into a dance—they chatted, reclined, and paddled, perfectly at home. She could feel the sunshine and the delightful breeze. As she looked, she felt a joy, something universal coming from the painting. Of course, she wasn't in the picture, but she took part in the joy of it—the splashing, the water, and the sunshine. The women would always be in the lovely summer light. In fact, they would be there even if she weren't there to look at them. Their joy would be there forever—maybe that's why people went to museums—to join something universal, for the vicarious experience.

Looking for somewhere else to sit down, Betty entered the newest wing of modern art. She looked around, puzzled; no bathers here, no landscapes.

"If that's art, you can have it!" Betty said, looking at a huge canvas that was mostly black.

"Let's see. What's this called?" said a voice behind her. "*Mother and Child*?"

She turned to see an older man looking amused. Betty peered at the title next to the picture. She had not meant to make the derogatory comment aloud. "It's called *Study 34*," she said.

"Of course. We should have guessed." He laughed. They both gazed at the picture. "Would you like it in your living room?"

"It certainly wouldn't fit, especially in my new one."

"You're moving?"

They turned to face each other. Betty saw he kept his remaining white hair very short on top and was wearing a tweed sport coat.

"Yes, to, ah," she regarded her companion who looked to be in his seventies, "to a retirement kind of place." She saw no point in making herself sound broken down to this gentleman.

"So you would need small pictures," he replied. "What kind would you like?"

"Well, not any of these." She looked around at the abstracts. Sharon had brought home pictures from kindergarten like that one on the far wall.

"Suppose we walk around and you pick out the ones you'd like," he suggested and took her arm. "Or maybe I'll try to sell you some of my favorites." They moved on to another group of rooms.

"Do you come here a lot?" In just a minute, she would pull her arm away.

"At least once a week. It's rather like church without the boredom of the service." He laughed. Betty knew exactly what he meant. It was how she felt looking at the bathers.

"The pictures do make you think and, well, feel awe," she agreed. "But I don't know anything about art."

"Come on, show me one you like."

She thought about the bathing women. Well, why not. She led him to it.

"Oh, you like the naughty ones," he said. "Of course, it's lovely. Isn't this too big for your living room too?"

"I guess I'll have to put it in the lobby. That will be a surprise for the administration." She thought of the orange and pink sunset in Monique's office.

"I'm sure it will be a hit. By the way, my name is Carlton."

"How do you do? I'm Betty." As they wandered into the American rooms, they established that he was from a Chicago suburb, and she was on a short visit to the city on her trip west.

"There's the pitchfork couple!" Betty said, surprised. She stopped to take a good look at the real thing. The farm couple was posed before their neat house, staring out of the picture, the woman with a worried expression. Betty knew that look well from her mother. Of course, their house hadn't been as orderly as this white one, with the snake plant on the porch, the wind blowing the sheer curtains. She walked up closer to get the details, then backed up and collided with Carlton.

"Did you know the painter, Grant Wood, had his dentist and his own sister pose for the picture?" he asked.

"Really? The man doesn't really look like a farmer, you know."

"Why not?"

"His skin is too perfect. Sun, wind, bitter cold, bug bites, it wears out skin fast. Then there are usually scars from a bolt flying loose or a fence wire snapping, some kind of accident like that. Farmers are often missing a finger or two, but that wouldn't have to show in the painting, of course."

"They look like a couple of sourpusses to me," Carlton said.

"I'm not surprised. Life on a farm is pretty hard. I grew up on a farm," Betty said. "One of my sisters stayed there until my father died. She looked about like that woman."

They sat down and looked at other pictures in the room until Carlton pointed out it was lunchtime and proposed they find a café.

"I brought my lunch, but I'd like some coffee to go with it," he said. Eleanor's Rosemary had packed Betty a sandwich, and coffee as a go-with sounded good.

"Let's go across Michigan to a place with a street view for people watching."

Betty grew nervous when she saw what he had in mind—one of those coffee places where they didn't seem to have regular coffee—but Carlton took her arm firmly and led them in.

"Now what would you like? My treat."

"I don't know, ah, just coffee?"

"Go ahead, pick something sinful."

Betty tried to interpret the list of drinks. *What was a café macchiato?* "Well, coffee with some cream in it."

"Here, allow me," he said, turning to the counter. "We'll have two mocha caramel lattes grande with lots of foam and two almond biscottis."

After whirring, swooshing, and stirring, a pretty girl served them up two coffees and long, brittle cookies. The bill was astonishing. Imagine paying for coffee what would get a whole lunch in Elkhart. They found a table in the window. Betty worried that it wasn't polite to unwrap their sandwiches, but she noticed other people had done the same.

"Coffee. Who could guess it could be so good?" said Carlton, taking a sip, and he laughed as he reached over to wipe some whipped cream off Betty's lip. Ordinarily, she would have been mortified, but it seemed completely natural. The coffee, chocolate, and caramel froth was heavenly rich.

"What is this called again? I would never remember all those words."

"Sure you would. It's a caramel mocha latte grande." He made her repeat it twice. Then he looked at this watch. "I've got to get to work."

"You have a job?"

"Today, I do. I'm an actor in movies and television."

"My goodness. I didn't realize." Betty wondered if he told all the women he met this. He was very self-assured. One man she knew at the senior center had told them he was a surgeon. It had been quite a while before someone recognized him as a tree trimmer, and this was after he had issued a lot of health advice.

"Now don't go getting overly impressed," Carlton said. "I'm an extra. You know all those people you see in a television or movie scene that add the atmosphere?"

"Aren't they just people who were there at the time?"

"Oh no. Those are us, the extras. We're hired to walk, sit, swim, die, or whatever, while the stars carry out their parts. Then later you watch the show or go to the movie and hope to see yourself in the scene."

"That's something. I never knew about that at all."

Betty had been in several plays in school and was a regular reader of *TV Guide*, *People*, and *Parade*. She had thought of joining community theater before Sharon was born but was afraid of embarrassing Charlie. It might not be good for business, after all.

"Lots of senior citizens are extras. You get paid, get free meals, if it's a full day or night. All you have to do is sign up with an agency, show up when they call you, and do whatever the scene calls for."

He told her about some of the movie stars he'd walked next to. He had even sat in a hot tub while Macaulay Culkin jumped into a hotel swimming pool years ago. "Believe me, I was a prune by the end of that shoot." Betty laughed and begged for more stories.

"Wait, why don't you come too? The scene is being shot right across the street. I know the agency PAs—that's production assistants—they will let you sign up right now. Please come, Betty. Wouldn't you like to be in a movie?" He looked her in the eye. "Come on, admit it."

"I do have to be at Union Station in the early evening for my train. I've already missed it two days in a row." Betty began to organize her purse and brocade bag. Suppose she made a fool of herself getting into something she didn't know anything about.

"This is a short shoot, so you'll have plenty of time. It's only noon now." He put his hand on her arm and squeezed it gently.

He was so enthusiastic and nice. *Of course* she'd like to be in a movie. It couldn't be worse than getting arrested, and certainly, Eleanor would do it if she had the chance.

"I guess it won't hurt anything. I'd love to." She took his arm as they neared the curb.

When they crossed Michigan Avenue in front of the Art Institute, they saw that crews had already set up a lot of equipment and barricades around a small park on the museum grounds. A crowd had already gathered hoping to see a star, and Carlton took them right through the crowd.

"Excuse us. Cast. Pardon us." The crowd parted like the Red Sea and someone asked them to pause for a photo. They edged their way around some dollies and over to a folding table where other extras crowded around, filling out paperwork. Carlton greeted a woman in a blue kerchief behind the table and asked to sign up Betty.

"You don't want to miss out on this lady. Isn't she perfect?"

"Just for you, Carlton, okay!" Without looking at Betty, she tossed her a form and W-9 to fill out. Betty fumbled as she tried to use a ballpoint pen on the uneven tabletop and wasn't sure of all the answers but didn't say so.

Handing in their paperwork, Carlton said, "There! Now you work for an agency! You're an actress. When you get a speaking part, you can join the Screen Actors Guild."

Betty felt her heart give a little flop, but a good kind. She looked around at the maze of power cords, the light bars, and the crew loaded down with tool belts and responding to two-way communication. She tried to focus: "Have you had a speaking part, Carlton?"

"I had to gurgle when a gangster shot me once, but that didn't count as speaking." He demonstrated a horrible death rattle, and Betty laughed and then apologized. He went on, "I'm still hoping for my big break. It's never too late, you know, in the business."

The business, it sounded so impressive, and she was part of it. Now this was something to tell Sharon, proof she wasn't just an old lady to put in assisted living. Not yet.

—∭—

While Betty was making her new acquaintance, Sharon and Vince wandered in North Michigan Avenue stores, enjoying themselves, though every quarter of an hour Sharon proposed yet another scenario for her mother's disappearance.

"Do you suppose Mother has reunited with an old boyfriend? A Shriner! Now why would she keep that a secret?"

Vince refrained from answering the question but agreed that this was a possible explanation.

This exchange occurred while they rested in chairs around a coffee-and-muffin kiosk in an atrium. Vince tipped his head back, and Sharon dug in her purchases to admire a kitschy pie spatula. When a woman sitting opposite began coughing, they focused attention on this companion, taking in the ratty shopping bags at her feet and her ill-fitting blue suit jacket and rakish hat.

Sharon nudged her own bags closer to her chair and put her purse handle back on her arm, but the woman's blue jacket and hat pierced her feigned disinterest in street people that was so easy to adopt in the city. She watched the woman rummage uselessly in her pockets as she coughed.

"Vince, do you think we should—"

"Maybe water?" He began to look around.

"We don't have a cup."

"Or, how about coffee? I'll go get coffee." Vince departed just as mall security arrived.

"These chairs are reserved for people buying coffee. You'll have to move along," he said, not addressing coffee-less Sharon. He moved away only after the woman stood up.

"Ma'am, wait, my husband went to get coffee for you."
The woman made no eye contact. "Here, take this." Sharon
held out a five-dollar bill, but she shuffled away.

Sharon watched the blue jacket recede through the
revolving door to the street. *What if I never find Mother?*
An appalling emptiness fought with a pettish refrain. *I don't
deserve this! Aren't I a good person?*

But no, a good person wouldn't lose her mother. If only
she had insisted on Shady Grove earlier, right after her
father's death, before her mother got, well, *different.* Then
she would have known Betty's whereabouts at that very
moment—maybe folding clean napkins for the dining room
with other residents, playing bunko, or watering the plants
in the greenhouse. Now, who knew where she was—maybe
she was alone on the street, her purse stolen (the navy blue
boxy one with big gold clasps) and confused over how to
get help. And, of course, she had no cell phone. (How many
times had they talked about that!)

Love for Betty filled her heart—her mother, her remaining mooring to the past, a person who had known her from
the beginning of time, someone who would love her uncon-
ditionally, like the mother of a murderer who says that boy
was her sweetest child.

Sharon and Vince shared the extra coffee and made
their way through more stores to the Michigan Avenue
Bridge where they waited while the roadbed rose for passing sailboats, then kept walking south to Millennium Park.
Vince, uneasy from the wall of tall buildings along the street,
wanted to sit under open sky to rest. Sharon pointed toward
Crown Fountain, which sounded restful. Then he discovered it wasn't a fountain at all, but a monster-sized water

park—two fifty-foot towers facing each other made of glass blocks. The blocks glowed fuchsia, then greenish, as they became waterfalls where water dribbled down from video greenery. Children splashed through the run-off, screaming with anticipation as a gigantic female face filled each tower edge to edge, eyes, brows, nostrils, and cheeks moving in slow-mo.

"Oh, isn't this clever?" Sharon said.

"Uh, sure. Very, uh, big." It was like standing way too close to someone.

Sharon got up to guide a wandering toddler back to his mother. Vince watched his wife's gestures, awkward since they had never had kids of their own. He felt bad. Maybe they should have gone to a university clinic here in Chicago instead of the doctors at home. Maybe someone could have fixed her problem.

"Cute little boy," Sharon said returning.

"Little boys and water—can't keep 'em apart."

"Do you think we would have been good parents?"

The question rattled him. Was this a question he was supposed to answer? Sometimes Sharon just talked and he wasn't supposed to answer, but now she was waiting, looking at him. So was the big face. *Don't say something dumb*, he counseled himself.

"You know how you hate dirt anywhere!" He decided to keep it light.

"I'm sorry about my shortcoming! You don't have to remind me."

Uh-oh, maybe this was a serious conversation. The eyebrow on the face rose slightly, watchful for his next move.

"Your problem wasn't a *shortcoming*. I never thought so, and my mother didn't either. Just something that, ah, happens." The eyes on the video screen widened.

"Your mother didn't either think *what* about *what*? What *shortcoming* are *you* talking about?" Sharon turned toward him watchfully. The glass block woman lowered her eyelids as her mouth began to slide into pursed lips.

"Honey, I didn't use that word. You did." He had stepped into it now and had to keep going, all the while seeing the giant lips moving toward a howl.

"I meant since we, uh, you couldn't have babies, I never held it against you. And my mother didn't either!"

"You told your mother I couldn't have children?" The eyes on the eavesdropper opened wide. Sharon too glanced at the interloper.

"I didn't want her to upset you by asking, so I told her."

"It's always the woman, isn't it?" Wife and giantess stared at him.

"Don't be mad, honey. I shouldn't have told her, I know."

"Especially since it's not true."

Finally, the fountain spewed! The boys screamed in faked surprise as the pursed lips sent out a fat spigot of water. Vince's surprise was not faked.

"But we went to that clinic. You had all the tests and everything."

"So did you. You just never checked on the results."

"But I assumed you found out it was a, a womanly condition." The faces had disappeared and the blocks spilled out water limply, like his dick, apparently. "Why didn't you tell me?"

"Really, Vince! You know how you are about stuff like that. Anyway, it would have been hard to fix."

He wished she had chosen a different word.

"I did a lot of reading about the condition."

Of course. Women always read up behind your back, just to keep a step ahead of you.

"Today, people would do in-vitro, but that wasn't common in our time."

Vince noticed they were holding hands and wondered when that had happened. She was right. Guys don't like doctors mucking around with their privates, so maybe she had been right not to tell him. A new face, a man this time, had appeared on the glass blocks, the expression sympathetic.

"Gotta tell you one more thing my mother said."

Even though he was over fifty, Sharon grabbed his collar and shook her finger in his face. "Let me guess. That you should have married a Catholic girl?"

"No, that I should love you anyway!"

"*Anyway*! That's just great, Vince."

He saw Sharon's usual expression of disgusted amusement with his mother, who these days wore a dumpy black shawl, dress, and stockings as had her mother before her.

"But I do. You know, love you. There was never any *anyway*."

He made an uncharacteristic move in public, taking his wife in his arms. Sharon pressed her cheek against his. Above them, the man smiled, openmouthed, as the water poured out.

19
Action!

*A*fter Betty and Carlton finished with the W-9 forms, they went to the holding area for extras where a nervous young woman quizzed them: "Have you got a wardrobe change? Wardrobe and makeup will be coming around in a few minutes."

"Yes, certainly," answered Carlton, holding up his own sports bag and Betty's paisley bag. Then he led Betty briskly over to the chairs surrounded by yellow tape.

"What have you got in this bag, Betty? Any clothes?"

The day was warmish, but Betty had topped off one of her new outfits with a light jacket of Eleanor's. "Yes, I have a few things." She wished she had taken the tags off. What if he thought she was a shoplifter!

"They may want to look at what you have, but don't show anything white or striped. It doesn't look good on-screen."

Betty, glad she hadn't put on what she now called her bumblebee outfit, surveyed the others who had gathered in holding, an assortment of races and ages. Some people played cards or read. One woman had set up artist materials and a gadget for pressing the art onto a pin-backed button.

"We'll have to get one of those before it's over," said Carlton. "You collect buttons for the movies you were in. See, she's getting paid as an extra and making more cash on the side."

"Well!" said Betty.

Carlton explained more about all the people in holding. The agency had put out a casting call for people of all ages. "This means if you bring your kids, they get paid, you get paid, and you all get at least one free meal." He had responded and the agency had called back to say he was hired. "Just another day in the business," he said, grinning.

Betty took in more details. There were canvas chairs marked Director just like you saw in the movies. *Well, this was the movies!*

Carlton nudged her. "Okay, here comes the PA and the wardrobe assistant to pick the actors. We want to get picked, so look alert."

My, he certainly knew just what to do. Betty sat up straight.

The PA walked through the chairs. "I need fifteen for the park scene. You, you and you—you got something you can cover that white shirt? Yes? Okay, you, yes, yes, the kids and their mom. Is he willing to ride in a stroller? Okay, you guys." She pointed and separated people, with the wardrobe assistant's approval. "Yeah, you Carlton, we'll need your hat, and, yes, your lady friend. We can do something with her. Come on everyone, we're running late."

Carlton's lady friend. That sounded nice.

He urged them along to the front of the pack. "There, we made it. The trick is be cooperative and wear something you think they'll like. See, I wore my aging professor outfit today since the setting is near the Art Institute," Carlton said. He pointed to his beret and corduroy jacket with a pipe in the pocket. "Sometimes I do sports fan or even street person."

"I guessed you were a retired teacher, the way you quizzed me about art." He was so well spoken too, but it would sound silly to mention that.

"Oh, sorry. I guess it never wears off, but I have been a house painter too. Mall greeter is still ahead of me."

"I hope not. Maybe you'll get your Hollywood break before that career!"

The wardrobe assistant looked them over. "Let's see what else you have here." She rummaged in Betty's bag. "No, this looks like cruise wear. You don't have a blue suit, by chance, something less stylish?"

"I'm sorry, no," said Betty. She thought of the last place she had seen her blue suit.

"Hey, bring me that blue jacket from the rack," the wardrobe assistant yelled to another assistant. Betty slipped into the jacket. It drooped at the shoulders in a familiar way.

"Yes, that's perfect. Now let me get you a walker."

"Oh, I can walk just fine."

Carlton poked her in the back.

"It's just a prop, lady. I want you two over there on that bench. Go."

"Never argue with an assistant or PA," said Carlton. "It's their job to make everything perfect for the scene. Then the director might notice a PA's work, and he or she will move up and get their own PA. It's really a dog-eat-dog sort of thing."

They moved to the bench and sat down next to a bed of orange and purple tulips. The sun warmed the small park. Passersby lingered on the other side of the yellow tape to watch them sit.

"Look at the people staring!" Betty said. "It's like we're in a picture in the museum! Oh, I feel so important." It was wonderful being on the inside of the yellow tape—legally this time.

"We are very important. We're background. After all, without us, there wouldn't be a scene."

"I do hope I don't forget my humble roots."

"No, don't become a diva, Betty. They're so insufferable!" His eyes were a watery blue, she noticed.

Then she practiced taking steps with her walker—she didn't want this gentleman to think she had one at home! They talked about their families, and Betty told him about her escape from assisted living.

"You're very brave!" he said after much laughter.

"Oh, just brave enough to do something dumb." She told about her near arrest. "I'm really not sure what I'll do next."

"I hope it will be wonderful." He smiled again.

The PA came back and showed everyone exactly what to do for the scene. Some people were to remain sitting, some were to walk quickly, and so on.

"Okay, there's going to be a motorcycle come through here with a stunt double on it. You don't have to be afraid. He won't hit you, but I want you to look startled. When you hear 'Background!' I want you to begin to move, just like I told you to. You're enjoying the park and are startled by the motorcycle. That's it. Nothing more."

"When do they tell us what this movie is about?" Betty whispered to Carlton.

"They don't. The plot is a secret, more or less. We're just background, remember?"

Just was too dismissive, Betty mused. Most of life is about background after all. You're always part of a tableau somewhere, and sometimes you're not sure what the real story line is. All you can rely on is what you understand is your role, without knowing whether you're playing out a script predestined by a Grand High Mystic Ruler or making your own choices within the general plot outline. Or, possibly, do we all act at random, freely, the director's chair being empty?

Well, that was certainly a big question that she would have to think about more. What she was certain about was that Shady Grove had been *holding*. Maybe this was the point of her trip: to prove that she wasn't too old to be background again, and even without a Screen Actor's Guild card, she could have a voice.

"Background!" Betty and Carlton heard their signal as a camera began rolling down a track to film the park. They looked toward each other, ignoring the moving dolly.

"Aaa-ction!" The director called. The scene came to life.

Carlton helped Betty to stand with her walker. "Remember, we're an old married couple having a day in the park," he said, then leaned over, and kissed her on the cheek.

It was delightful! "You think this scene might be your lucky break to Hollywood?" Betty murmured, mindful of her role as lady friend.

"Yes, it just might be. A romantic lead! You know, they'll have to shoot this about a dozen times today. My lips may get chapped!"

"Well, I just may get spotted for those female roles of doddering old lady. Katharine Hepburn and Jessica Tandy are dead now, of course."

"Doddering but beautiful," said Carlton.

"Or perhaps doddering but rich?" Betty's eyes sparkled.

"No, those women are such dragons," said Carlton firmly folding her hand over his arm.

Just then they heard the motorcycle and turned to look as it raced by less than a dozen feet from them. Betty yanked her walker out of the way, and Carlton steadied her and shook his fist at the cycle. The scene was over in seconds.

"Cut!"

The PAs walked around making a few adjustments after the director gave more instructions. "Good, people. Let's not look too surprised. It's not a nuclear bomb, just a motorcycle. I like the walker action, ma'am, good job. Places!"

Carlton explained this meant they were to go back to the starting point. For the next hour, they returned again and again and ran through the scene. "Take 6. Take 7." The production people really did use one of those snappers with the take number written on it, Betty noted. The extras even got a break where Carlton took her to the craft table for lemonade and brownies. They discovered the male lead had arrived, as handsome in person as on the screen.

"Do we get an autograph?" This would be something to show her bridge girls and Sharon.

"No, it's considered bad style to even wave or stare. We're all working together."

—⚡—

After Crown Fountain, Sharon led Vince along Michigan Avenue to the Art Institute, avoiding the soaring pedestrian bridge out of Millennium Park. They paused with other bystanders to watch what was happening in a little park full of equipment and cameras. Perhaps it was a breaking news story, they said. A motorcycle tore through the park just missing an older couple. The onlookers cheered.

"Vince, my God, there's Mother!" Sharon grabbed his sleeve. "What is she doing there? Why, she's been hurt! She has a walker."

Nothing could surprise Vince at this point. He stared into the park as Sharon went on, "All that dancing! She probably fell. And who's that man she's with?"

"Maybe a Shriner?"

Sharon wormed her way to the yellow tape. "Mother! Mother! Over here!"

The voice of her child filtered through all other sounds to Betty. Oh, she had so much to tell Sharon but not now. Instead, she waved gaily but turned away.

"Mother, what are you doing? Mother! We've been so worried." Sharon ignored glares from other women who were trying to stay up front.

"Background!" Betty and Carlton got up, and he leaned to kiss her cheek.

"Action." They began their walk.

"Mother! You're hurt!" screamed Sharon.

"Don't bother me now!" Betty yelled without turning her head. She couldn't ruin the scene. They heard the motorcycle.

"Watch out for that motorcycle!" It roared past and Betty pulled her walker out of the way.

"Mother! Come over here right now!" The yellow tape strained as Sharon pushed forward.

"Places!" Carlton and Betty returned to the bench, with Carlton carrying the walker.

"I can't talk to you. We might miss our cue." Betty pointed to the director.

"What are you talking about? What cue? How did you get hurt?"

"I'm not hurt. That's my prop." Betty took the walker from Carlton and waved it. "I'm working. I'm in this movie."

"Background! Action!" The motorcycle went through again. Then Betty was able to turn toward her family.

"But you can't get a job. You're in assisted living." Sharon began to twist the buttons on her jacket, Betty noticed. She and Charlie had tried so hard to discourage her tendency to fidget with her hands.

"Sharon! Go away. We'll talk later."

"But, Mother." Sharon seemed oblivious to the onlookers listening to this interchange.

"Sharon, both of you *go into the museum*." Betty watched Vince scan the imposing building. "You don't have to know anything about art," she shouted. "Just look!"

"Tell them to come back in an hour. It will be a wrap by then. We're only being paid until three today," Carlton said.

Betty raised her voice. "We're going to wrap at three. Vince, meet us at that coffee shop, the one with the Italian name." Betty pointed across the street. "We'll have a latte."

"Take 10. Background, and aaa-ction!" the director shouted. The park sprang into movement, Carlton kissed,

Betty smiled and took baby steps with her walker, the motorcycle roared. Vince admired the skill of the driver as his mother-in-law expertly whipped her walker out of the cycle's path.

Sharon said, "Meet her for a *latte*?"

20
Charlie's Surprise: Take 2

Sharon nearly knocked over her coffee in her haste to embrace her mother when Betty and a man entered the café. Betty squeezed her daughter gently for several seconds. Seeing Sharon and Vince was like putting on a bathrobe after a long day—comforting, yes, but now you couldn't go out. Coveting a few more free minutes, she asked Carlton to order her a mocha caramel latte, her second that day.

"Nice to meet you both." Carlton shook hands warmly. His presence deterred complex explanations and recriminations, as Betty had hoped. She described their becoming acquainted in the museum and her performance as an extra. Sharon and Vince smiled tensely.

"We've had quite an afternoon. They did about a dozen takes on just a couple of scenes, getting the motorcycle from several angles. Your mother is a natural!"

"Yes, playing an old lady was such a challenge." Betty gestured grandly.

Betty was careful not to say "lady friend" to Sharon. Poor Sharon. It was hard for her to get a grip, but who could blame her: *Escaped mother found on movie set*. Well, there would be plenty of time to make it up to her and Vince for the worry and expense, perhaps give them a gift certificate to eat out at a fancy place at home.

"Betty, the set PA wants us for another scene tomorrow. Can you make it?" She felt Carlton addressing her.

Sharon reached for Betty's bag. "But Mother, now that we've found you, you can come home with us. Actually, Vince would like to leave today before the traffic gets heavy." He put down his chocolate brownie obediently to scan his watch.

"No, I can't leave now. I have an appointment at a bank at four thirty today."

"Bank? What are you talking about now, Mother?"

Really, did Sharon have to treat her like an imbecile in front of Carlton? "Your father left some business to take care of here in a bank." *There, that was simple and true, or true enough.* "That's why I'm in Chicago, dear." She beamed at Sharon and took back the paisley bag.

Carlton stood up. "It's a big scene with the leads tomorrow morning in Union Station. You'll be working with the stars! Oh, the PA said to bring something different to wear. Do you have a navy suit, by chance?"

The same reckless feeling was coming over Betty as at NuLook Salon, Mabel's Pontiac, and the protest. Or maybe it was just so much coffee.

She looked at Carlton: "Oh, well, the last time I saw mine, it was hanging on a hook at the Drake!"

Sharon's expression was priceless.

"Here's my number. Just give me a call. I hope to see you tomorrow in the station lobby. You'll see the registration table." He wrote his number on a napkin.

"Do you think the craft people will have the chocolate-chip brownies again?" Insider jargon felt so good that she longed for more, but with Sharon and Vince here it would be unconscionable not to go home with them.

"With doughnuts and croissants too in the morning!" He gave her shoulder a squeeze. "Nice to meet you folks." He shook hands with Vince. Betty saw his tweed jacket recede into the crowd on the street.

For a few minutes more, Betty and Sharon exchanged the highlights of the last thirty-six hours, with Betty and Vince making no reference to the protest escapade.

Though she tried to discourage Sharon and Vince from coming with her to the bank, they insisted and flagged down a taxi outside the coffee shop. Vince got up front with the driver.

"It may be confusing, Mother. We'll be there to help you figure out about the lockbox," Sharon said as she maneuvered the paisley bag into the back seat and fussed about Betty's stepping off the curb.

"I think I know what a lockbox is."

Though Betty was glad to see her, of course, Sharon was getting on her nerves. And, sadly, she couldn't help but notice how Sharon and Vince looked like country mice in their matching, red, zip-up jackets.

"Do you have the lockbox key, Mother?"

"No, but Eleanor said they will just charge a fee for a new one."

"Who told you that? Oh, yes, Eleanor, your new acquaintance."

Betty could tell that Sharon didn't think much of her mother having made a close friend in the city. For Sharon, the whole thing would be further proof of her needing the supervision of assisted living now that she was discussing personal business with strangers.

The cab deposited them in front of a grey, imposing structure just off LaSalle Street. The security guard blocked their entrance. "Clients only," he said. Sharon and Vince hesitated, but Betty spoke up, "I have an appointment with Mrs. Graveswell."

He passed them along to another security person in a marble lobby, this time a young man in a grey suit and red tie. This was a far cry from First Whatever at home where security was a tape measure glued to the inside frame of the exit door. Across the lobby, a staircase rose to meet the twinkling of heavy chandeliers suspended over the room at the top.

"How may I help you, madam?" The young man smiled at Betty.

"I have a meeting about my late husband's lockbox." Betty glanced at the flight of marble steps ahead.

"You must be looking for Mrs. Graveswell. Take the first elevator on your left, main floor."

He rushed to press the button and they stepped in. Betty could hear heavy breathing from Vince as they went up, the ponderous speed of the elevator confirming the rarefied air of these surroundings. They trooped into a grand salon only recognizable as a bank by a few walnut teller windows and rows of desks where smart-looking bankers chatted quietly with a few clients. They were waved toward the vaults where Betty stated her business to another assistant who deposited Sharon and Vince in chairs outside a gated area. In moments a petite woman in an elegant grey suit ushered Betty inside the gate and ordered the assistant to help Betty slip off her jacket and bring her a glass of iced cucumber water.

"I'm Mrs. Graveswell." The woman extended her hand. "You must be Mrs. Miles."

It was quite astonishing to be addressed by someone who called herself Mrs. and extended the same courtesy to Betty. In this bank people knew how to behave with old-fashioned courtesy.

"I would like to take care of some business."

Betty unsnapped the center clasp on her purse, found the letter, and handed it over. Mrs. Graveswell put on gold half glasses and read it over. Betty noted that her desk was almost bare—no collection of branded coin banks or ceramic elephants. There was a folder and a framed formal photo of children and presumably Mr. Graveswell and herself. Idly, Betty wondered what her first name was—what could sound good with Graveswell?—but her nameplate was angled wrong for viewing.

"I am so sorry to hear of your loss, Mrs. Miles. We have wondered what had happened to Chuck, that is, Mr. Miles."

Through her officious condolence came a note of sincerity, a nice touch compared to the tedious offers of prayers, pies, and just-let-us-know-if-we-can-do-anything comments she had endured for her first year of widowhood.

"Yes, *Charles* passed away four years ago last January."

"That accounts for our not seeing him, certainly."

"He was here often?" Betty glanced around the room, unable to picture her husband in this environment.

"I wouldn't say often, but he was quite a favorite of some of us over the years."

"I see." That she could picture. He had always had a way with other men's wives in the Elks too. But just in good fun. This woman was the type he liked—a champagne blond (dyed, of course) and makeup with a dressy look. Betty pondered these details, trying to gauge the age of this fashion plate.

"We always wanted to meet you." She looked at Betty over her glasses.

Busy with Sharon at first, then cautioned by Charlie that the city was dirty and unsafe, Betty had rarely come with him, especially right before he retired since he rode with other fellows from the district office. Two of them were dead now and the third a widower.

"Now, Mrs. Graveswell, if you don't mind, I'd like to have the box." Betty moved to the edge of her chair.

Back home at First Whatever, you just signed a little card and went into the safe with the bank girl. She would shove your key into the box, then, often as not, it took her a few tries to find the proper matching bank key. Then you took your box into one of two tiny rooms like a restroom stall, sat down on a rickety chair, and conducted your business as fast as possible.

"Of course, Mrs. Miles. I understand completely that you would like to settle this. Now, we do have many security measures. Do you have identification and perhaps his death certificate?"

Mrs. Graveswell was all business. In spite of her equating officiousness with phoniness, Betty admired Mrs. Graveswell's proficiency with her computer, her fingers flying at the keys with rings sparkling while she was glancing at documents over her half glasses. Twice, just a flit of her hand sent a young man racing to a printer. Finally, the paperwork was in order, after Betty wrote a check for replacing the missing key. As they moved into a vault that reminded Betty of a columbarium, she could see Sharon starting to stand, but she did not invite her through the little gate. An assistant carried keys and went up a ladder as Mrs. Graveswell pointed to the proper container where both keys glided in without fussing. They all paraded down a discrete hallway toward a half dozen doors. The assistant unlocked a door and backed out as Mrs. Graveswell gestured.

"Now, I'll just leave you here, Mrs. Miles. Stay as long as you like. Would you like more water? Coffee?" She pulled out a chair at a mahogany desk for Betty in a miniature and silent office. "Just press this buzzer if you need anything."

The door closed and Betty was alone with the metal box, slightly burnished and remarkably similar to the container of Charlie's ashes. She sat down, overwhelmed by unease. It was too late to not come here at all, but she could just chuck the box contents into an envelope, as a problem to deal with later.

What to do?

She fumbled through her wallet to find a photo she carried of their fiftieth wedding anniversary. She wanted to examine Charlie's expression, somber, if she recalled the photo correctly, and he stared to the left slightly, rather than at the camera. His arm was around her shoulder where an

orchid was pinned—she had been surprised with the cor-
sage he had bought her for the dinner party at the Elks.

She held the photo under a green-shaded lamp on the
desk. He seemed to be looking more at the camera than she
recalled, so his eyes met hers fully now, and there was the
hint of the raised eyebrow in spite of the serious lips. She
moved the photo from side to side, but the sight line was
the same. Well, obviously, the green shade on the lamp was
doing something funny with the photo. He looked downright fearful.

She brushed her hand on the box. It's now or never to
open it. If a heart attack were to result, she could press the
darned buzzer. She turned the box latch and tipped up the
lid. Inside at the front end was a velvet box like a gift from
a jeweler's. Though her heart knocked dangerously, she
resisted opening it first. Instead, she pulled out a couple of
long envelopes. Unsealing one, she discovered government
savings bonds dated from the last thirty years. She riffled
through the stack, counting the small denominations that
had long ago matured.

Thirty thousand dollars! Betty gasped.

They had scrimped at home while he had been in
Chicago buying bonds! An enclosed note in her husband's
hand read, *For Sharon.* How nice for their daughter, the
apple of his eye, for certain. The box was turning out
to be a treasure trove. Her resentment over their thrift
dissolved.

A second envelope about the same size had a lesser
amount; ten thousand, she counted. Well, Charlie always
did love to surprise Sharon. This was the ultimate surprise,

surely, and quite like him to keep them in the dark about a decision, even one that would please. And what was he waiting for, a grandchild? Sharon had passed forty while he held onto this box. Betty glanced at his photo again but the sense of the meeting eyes was gone. He clearly was staring over her shoulder. As she was combining the two envelopes, another note in his hand dislodged from the bonds: *For Irene.*

Irene? Betty rummaged through names of her husband's close female relatives: Marcella, Connie, Lynne, but no Irene. The flutter of pleasure turned to rage.

She gulped the glass of water, swallowing the wrong way and choking. Soon there came a discrete knock at the door. "Mrs. Miles? Are you all right?"

Betty gasped out, "Uh-ha," but her throat was so graveled by the cough, she couldn't speak at first.

"Shall I get your daughter?" Mrs. Graveswell opened the door a crack.

"Certainly not! I'm fine, thank you. I'll be out soon." Betty thought of the photo with its eyebrow smothered under the placemats at Shady Grove and their anniversary photo in front of her with its shifty eyes. She wrenched open the delicate clasp on the velvet box. Inside was a necklace, a diamond on a gold heart pendant.

"For *Irene,* Charlie?" Betty said. Then looking closely, she read, "Love to my Betty for sixty golden years."

No, they didn't quite make it to sixty years. "I'm going to put it on," Betty told the anniversary photo, and when she closed the fastener around her neck the pendant fell perfectly over her collar bone into the heart-shaped crevice where Charlie had so often planted a kiss.

"Oh, Chipper, what did you do? Why aren't you here to explain?" Her loss fell on her sharply, freshened by the mysterious woman.

She fingered the pretty pendent. It was hard to imagine Charlie, who felt jewelry was wasteful, buying such a lovely—and obviously costly—necklace. It was beautifully engraved too. Was it just to take away guilt over Irene?

Some wives would have crumpled the photo, but Betty put it back in her purse. She sighed and shoved the savings bonds in her purse, center section. And snapped it shut. *Didn't the Queen too have to sweep indiscretions under the rug in the past?* She left the little sanctuary, heading toward Mrs. Graveswell's desk.

"Would you like to extend the rental on the box, Mrs. Miles?"

"No, there's no need."

"In that case, let me just ask for your signature here, and I'll print a receipt for the closure. Do sit down while I go get the paperwork." This time, because Betty took the other chair by the desk, the nameplate was pointed her way: Irene Graveswell.

The chandeliers sparkled knowingly overhead.

The gargantuan door on the vault yawned. *Oh, it was an old story. The wife is the last to know.*

And what was there to know? She would find out when Mrs. Graveswell returned. Betty set her purse on the desk, turning her attention to the photo on the desk.

"Your grandchildren?" she asked when Irene returned.

"Oh no. That's us back when the children were younger. It's kind of silly to keep such an old photo here, but we looked so happy in that one."

"That's *Mr.* Graveswell?"

She nodded. "Here you are, Mrs. Miles." Mrs. Graveswell held out the receipt. "Do let me know if there is anything else we can do for you."

Such as borrow a husband? Too late for any more of that. Betty glanced at Sharon and Vince who were now strolling around, looking at a wall of photos in a distant alcove.

"Actually, I have something for you." Betty placed the savings bonds with their note in front of Irene. "These were in the safe deposit box. It seems you knew my husband rather well, I gather."

Irene gasped before she burst into tears, dabbing at her careful makeup.

"Oh, yes. He was so kind for years."

Mrs. Graveswell tried to hide her breakdown from the younger associates by ducking down to look in a drawer. Betty reached for tissues from a nearby desk, handing them in bunches to the sobbing woman. "Oh, I have missed him so much," she said.

"I don't think I want to hear all the details." This was ridiculous.

"But I want you to know. I've wanted to tell you for a long time—but I didn't want to just write out of the blue. Of course, I checked for a death notice when we didn't hear from him."

Of all the nerve. Betty had met silly, self-centered women before, but this was astonishing—at her advanced age weeping like a jilted teenager in the presence of the wife.

"Chuck always said he would tell you. That you would take it well. Oh, I felt so terrible when I realized I would never see him again." Her mascara was running south.

Betty handed her another tissue. She kept waiting for someone to yell "Cut" and "Take 2," but this was real life and not to be done over. Eleanor had said it was time to find out if he was a prince or a prick. Well, now she knew.

"Now, now, Irene. We all lose someone sometime. Just take the bonds he wanted you to have." Betty got up to leave, closing her purse and putting on her jacket.

"Oh, don't go. I want you to hear the whole thing."

She led Betty back to the little room where, amid more tears, she explained how they had met when she was the telephone operator at his corporate office, how her own husband was a reckless lush, how when Charlie discovered her husband carried no insurance . . . naturally—

"He paid for a whole life policy, because I just couldn't afford it," she sobbed. "And sure enough, my husband fell in front of the L train." She gestured his demise with her hands. Then she had gotten a job at this bank, and Chuck—such a gentleman—checked on her from time to time when he was in town. It had been a struggle, even with the insurance money, raising children, and had it not been for Chuck's attention, well—Betty listened patiently through this recital of facts, those cited and those no doubt omitted.

"I'm sure *Charlie* would have wanted you to have the bonds, so you keep them. I don't need them," Betty couldn't help adding. She flipped open her new little jacket to reveal its good label.

"Oh, I couldn't, after meeting you," Irene murmured.

"Well, I couldn't either."

Betty got up without putting a steadying hand on the nearby desk, as she would have done ordinarily. "You must have grandchildren you could give them to."

"Yes, of course. The last one is in college. That would be helpful."

The women went back to the main room where Sharon and Vince were coming toward them, red jackets bunched in Vince's right arm, his left around his wife. Betty bundled them off before an extended encounter with Irene could occur, and to Sharon's inquiry about the woman's obvious tears, she replied, "She's just touched that I'm a widow. Silly woman."

21
Betty's Surprise: Take 1

The street noise made it impossible to talk about the lockbox on the sidewalk in front of the bank. The five o'clock crowd surged around them as they stood undecided about where to go, but the security guard spotted an empty cab and they got in. Vince looked to Sharon for their destination.

"Union Station," she ordered. "That's where the car is and Mother can pick up her suitcase."

Sharon took Betty's hand in the backseat. At last, the ordeal was over. She was moving from irritation to amusement over her mother's escapade. "I can't imagine where you've been!" she said. "I'll want to hear all about everything on the way home." The details would surely entertain her colleagues, now that her mother was secured again.

Betty barely listened to Sharon's account of their search for her as she thought about the bank encounter. The unwieldy problem—Charlie's perfidy—she folded corner to corner, so it could be shoved in a drawer for consideration later. The other issue was simple and could be dealt with today.

Vince, mindful of heavy traffic, suggested they sit for a while at a café and leave after six. They ordered iced tea and cheese fries.

"What about the safe deposit box?" Sharon asked again. She wondered if her mother had forgotten a manila folder or envelope at the bank. "Were there business papers in it?"

"Actually, yes." Rejuvenated by the drippy fries, Betty was anxious to deliver Charlie's surprise—now her surprise. "They're for you."

"For me? Where are they?"

"Right here in my purse." Betty snapped open the clasp for the center compartment and laid the long envelope of bonds in front her daughter and son-in-law. "These are for you to open a business."

The bonds had the same effect on Sharon as on Mrs. Graveswell. Vince reached for the napkins at a nearby table to sop up tears. Betty showed Sharon her necklace, which brought out a fresh sprinkling from both women. Vince doled out more napkins.

"Why here in Chicago? Didn't Daddy have a safe deposit box at home?"

"Well, your father had his own ideas about the way to do some things, you know." This would be sufficient detail for the time being.

From where they sat in the twilight, Betty could see the lights shining row upon row in the Willis Tower—she was getting used to the new name. The water taxi delivered commuters to the station and a sightseeing boat made a turnaround in the bluish-pink evening light. On a napkin,

Sharon outlined the plan for a catering business she and Vince had talked about. He described an old storefront that would be perfect. Betty noted their shared excitement. *Yes, every marriage needed a third leg and this could be theirs*, she mused.

After they got Betty's bag from rail storage, they walked back into the Grand Hall. Already the camera dollies were being set up for tomorrow and parts of the floor were blocked off. Betty halted their little parade toward the parking garage.

"I'm not going with you, dear." Freedom had to be now or never.

"You don't have to go back to assisted living, Mother. I want you with us."

"Oh, never mind that. I want to stay here in the city for now. Eleanor needs me."

"But I—we—need you."

"Not now. You and Vince need to see about renting a building. Besides, I'm working tomorrow, remember?" She smiled at her daughter.

"Mother, really!" Sharon felt a wave of familiar exasperation, but she held back further retorts. "If that's what you want, I guess I understand." She saw an unfamiliar expression on her mother's face—determination. Vince laughed because they both had their arms crossed, duck pose.

"Yes, it's what I want."

"What about cash? Vince can use the ATM for you."

"Don't worry about that. I'll just live on plastic."

Vince grinned as Betty elbowed him. Poor old Sharon, it was going to be hard for her to let go. "I'm just making up for lost time, dear." Betty hugged her daughter.

Joyce Hicks

"Here, take my cell phone at least, so you can call." Betty moved her purse in front of her stomach again. "No complaints, Mother. I can still be bossy on some things."

Betty held out her hand for the phone as if being handed a frog. "I suppose I'm the last woman in the state to get one. Now, which one of these dinky buttons do you push to phone someone?" Sharon reviewed the steps and waited while her mother called Eleanor, who lived on Lake Shore Drive of all places.

"Is the guest suite still available, or should I go to the Drake?" Betty said when Eleanor answered. Sharon rolled her eyes.

"We've kept it just for you! So, tell me, was he a prince or a prick?"

The rhyme about Peter and the pickled peppers popped into Betty's head. Now she knew the answer to the last line: *Where's the peck of pickled peppers Peter Piper picked?*

"Ah, both I think. I'll tell you everything soon," she said, then regretted such a promise in front of her Sharon.

But really, there were some things to be shared only with a friend.

Acknowledgments

*N*ovels grow with the encouragement of others. I thank *Literary Mama* for accepting "An Outing for Betty" for publication in 2007 and Kristina Riggle, fiction editor for *Literary Mama* and novelist, for encouragement when the story had turned into a novel.

Blank Slate writers, Valparaiso, Indiana, have been great friends and listeners. Kathleen Marlowe, a good friend, made many plot suggestions as we swung around a walking track on our lunch hour. Author Stephanie Wilson Medlock cheered for Betty as we sent chapters back and forth and shared many excellent lunches; may this fulfilling relationship continue.

Editor Kelly Finefrock-Creed was invaluable in editing and polishing. Thank you so much for your stylistic suggestions and careful reading. Lastly, colleague and passionate reader Cynthia Rutz gave great help on chapter titles and other niceties.

I couldn't have written *Escape from Assisted Living* without inspiration from the company of older women who find ways to expand their horizons at any age.

Author bio

For over 35 years Joyce Hicks worked with student writers at a midwestern university and on occasion was a film extra in Chicago. Her stories have appeared in *Passager, Touch: The Journal of Healing, Literary Mama, Uncharted Frontier,* and others. She lives in northwest Indiana with her husband and pets. They have a summer place in northern Michigan, where their grandchildren love to visit.

Visit joycebhicks.com.

One More Foxtrot, a tale of second chances

Sequel to *Escape from Assisted Living*

What does it take to forgive, move on, or rekindle romance?

The year after 80-year-old Betty Miles' exit from senior living *(Escape from Assisted Living)*, she's happy staying in Chicago with friend Eleanor. She's dating, making new friends, and reconnecting with an old one. Her daughter Sharon D'Angelo is busy with her new dessert shop in Elkhart, Indiana, funded by a legacy from her father. Good feelings between Betty and Sharon may be short-lived after a stranger makes an astonishing claim. Will mother and daughter work through this mystery together? *Of course not.* They have kept upsetting truths secret their entire lives.

With her hands full—clients making moves on her husband Vince, her mother-in-law meddling in the desserts, and a visitor sleeping over—Sharon keeps her mother away. Timing isn't right for revelations of the goings-on in Elkhart. Meanwhile, Betty's sleuthing family history, keeping her suspicions secret like a good wife and mother. But when past transgressions come to light, Betty finds out whether truth will enhance or destroy her family.

Finalist, Next Generation Indie Book Awards, 1st Place National Federation of Press Women, fiction

Unexpected Guests at Blackbird Lodge

Charlotte often agonizes over her unfinished novel, picturing a different life than innkeeper with her husband Will. Too late she's informed a man from her past, a sexy noted author, will star in a writers' workshop she booked to shore up the lodge finances. Their reunion and a secret Charlotte might be compelled to reveal will spark domestic fireworks or the fulfillment of old dreams.

How could a week get any more complicated?

More surprises—another ex's arrival, an unsolved murder revived, coded guestbook messages, and daughter Alice's woke requests. Charlotte has her hands full, all while hiding an emotional roller-coaster ride as the lodge oozes with creative and erotic vibes.

Will Charlotte be able to salvage her marriage by the time the week is over? *Will she want to?*

Made in the USA
Middletown, DE
25 July 2024